ALSO BY THE AUTHOR

First Valentine (Kit & Tully Book 2)
First Album (Kit & Tully Book 3)

Kit & Tully

Book 1

FIRST KISS

Mocha Von Bee

First published in 2022 by Indie Ink

Copyright © 2022 MochaVon Bee

The moral right of the author has been asserted.

All characters and events in this publication are fictitious and any resemblance to real persons, living or dead, is purely coincidental.

All rights reserved. No part of this publication may be reproduced or transmitted in any form or by any means, electronic or mechanical, including photocopying, recording, or any information storage or retrieval system, without prior permission in writing from the publishers.

ISBN: 978-1-7392353-0-7

Printed and bound by Lightning Source

Cover design by S.E.Anderson

To Tom, who's always believed that the whole point of dreams is to make them come true.

First Letter From Aonghus

Dear Reader,

Over the course of this series, you will meet a cast of characters, a group of friends and some random acquaintances, who over time become more closely connected, as their paths intertwine.

You will come to understand them all, root for some and object to others. There will be romance and there will be death. It may be murder, or perhaps fate, possibly a combination of the two. Don't worry about it now, there's plenty of time to watch it all unfold, form your own theories and draw your own conclusions.

At some point, even I can be found within these pages, and, like the characters in this story, you too can choose whether or not to believe in me.

Before I begin I must be clear. This is not my story. It's the story of a young couple who woke me. It's not that simple though, because only one of them believed they'd woken me.

Our story starts with the optimistic outsider who has just arrived and has no idea how wrong he is about everything he sees.

Please meet the hapless New Guy, Tully Cabe.

Yours,
Aonghus

Chapter 1

The door cracks open and a girl peeps out, eyes sweeping the vicinity. Flanked by doric pillars and capped with an ornate fanlight, it's the kind of door that's never open to me. This is the nice part of town. A flight of granite steps leads up to the door and the traditional red paint is fresh and bright against the greyness of the day and the imposing stone facade. How does it feel to be wealthy enough to live behind a door like that? Do all your worries disappear when you've that kind of solidity to protect you from the outside world?

I wait for her to emerge under a large umbrella, in one of those expensive trench coats rich girls wear. Instead a flurry of booted, swirling black eases through the door, closing it soundlessly behind her. She has a small, collapsible umbrella. She struggles for a moment to open it, then with a final furtive glance, offering a glimpse of a white heart-shaped face and red lipstick, she darts down the steps and disappears around a corner.

Just then, the church bell tolls, its loud clang making me jump. It's a big church, almost a cathedral, and its soaring spire is the main landmark of the town. The sound vibrates into the air, reminding me I need to hurry. I can't be late for my first day in the new job.

In the grey drizzle, everything blends together. Like most Irish towns, the main street of Drimshanra is long and lined with bumper to bumper traffic. June is almost over but the weather has been so cold and unrelenting that summer still feels so far off. In fact, I'm beginning to wonder if it somehow bypasses the town completely.

A short cut leads along the river past empty stretches of derelict warehouses, but I don't like going into town that way. Covered in graffiti, the boarded up buildings remind me of where I've come from. Walking down Main Street takes longer but feels safer.

As soon as I pass through the automatic doors, the comforting warmth of the town shopping centre welcomes me inside and I make my way to More Video 4U with a smile on my face. My watch and the big clock over the centrally located café both tell me I'm ten minutes early, which is exactly what I've aimed for. It's important to make a good first impression, especially since jobs are so hard to find in Drimshanra and I'm on a trial period.

More Video 4U is a large unit down one of the side aisles. A bell chimes as I push the door open and Andy, the manager, looks up.

"Tully Cabe, right?" he smiles when he sees me, "Here, I'll show you what to do."

I follow him through the racks of video files as he explains how they are arranged.

"We put all the sleeves back on the shelves when they come in," he explains, "that way our customers know what we have in stock. If there's no sleeve on the shelf, it means all the copies are out. Of course, most of the time we only have one copy, unless it's a big hit."

I nod. It's all familiar to me because I've grown up going to various branches of More Video 4U and they all look the same – large and brightly lit, aisles arranged by genre. Thrillers, classics, romcom, noir, whatever mood you're in, whatever kind of film you like, the promise of escape is always there, waiting for you.

"And remember," Andy's voice turns urgent, "if

somebody hasn't got their membership card, no matter what excuse they give you, you can't let them have a video."

"Right!" I nod, but he must catch a trace of doubt in my voice because the smile leaves his face.

"I'm serious, kid. People will tell you anything, and some of the excuses will break your heart, but they're only scamming. It's more than your job's worth to listen to them."

Then he takes me behind the counter to show me the drawers where the videos are stored and explain how to use the cash register and the computer with the customer database.

"But if all their information is in here, surely we can just check who they are if they forget their card?"

"Yeah?" Andy says. "Okay, my name is Sean Costello and I live at 17 Ardmore Close."

Yes, I tap a few keys on the computer, eager to show Andy the one thing I do know how to do. "Found you!"

"Except I'm not Sean Costello," he shakes his head sadly, "place like this, where everyone is broke, petty theft is rampant. People borrow under someone else's name and we never see the video again. So yeah, make sure they have their card!"

"Right," I feel like I've failed a test, "got it."

The afternoon is quiet. Mainly groups of schoolgirls dropping in to browse and giggle in the aisles. They leave without getting anything.

"Lots of youngsters like hanging out in here, makes them feel grown up," Andy explains, "but they are better for business than you might think because they always find something they want to watch, and then they pester somebody to rent it for them later on, another reason we need to be particular about cards. Listen, I'm going to slip out for a while, before it gets busy."

"Oh!" I wasn't expecting to be left on my own as soon as this.

"Are you able to do the job or not?" An edge enters his voice.

"Sure, I think I've got the hang of it." It's not the job is difficult, just I haven't had much chance to practise yet.

"That's what I like to hear," Andy slaps my shoulder. "There's plenty of people looking for a handy number round here." This time the threat isn't veiled.

"Take as long as you like. I'll be fine."

"Good man, Tully!" He nods in approval.

He's only gone ten minutes when the girl I saw coming out of her house earlier enters the shop and shakes off her umbrella. It didn't do much to keep her dry. Her jeans are plastered to her legs and I look away quickly in case she thinks I'm staring.

She heaves a deep sigh and I remember my job.

"Hey," I step out from behind the counter, "how can I help you?"

"Just looking," she replies.

"A copy of Titanic has just come back." I'm pleased with myself for thinking of it. Copies of Titanic are like gold dust.

"Are you seriously trying to be helpful?" She rolls her eyes, turns into one of the aisles and stares at the Pick of the Week section.

"How about that?" I point at a Men in Black poster. If she doesn't like Titanic, maybe she'd prefer something funny and offbeat.

But she's already seen it.

It's becoming clear she doesn't want to talk to me and I don't want her to think I'm harassing her.

"You're not from here, are you?" she asks as I edge away.

"No." I stop in my tracks. "We just moved down. From Dublin."

"What do you think of Drimshanra?"

That's a hard question to answer. Even though I hardly know the town at all yet, my first impressions couldn't be described as positive, but she lives here and I'd hate to sound critical of her home.

"It's different, takes a bit of getting used to." I glance around, desperate to change the subject. "Here, you might like this." I hand her a video sleeve, 'LA Confidential' with Russell Crowe and Kim Basinger. "It's darker."

She shakes her head and moves on, leaving me standing in the middle of the aisle, not sure if I've been dismissed or if I should follow her, when I hear her call, "I'll take this one."

She pulls down a copy of 'Strictly Ballroom' and brings it over to me.

"Nice," I say with a smile I hope is professional, "excellent choice! That finale, the way he slides out across the dance floor. It has to be one of the best entrances ever."

I take the sleeve from her and bring it over to the cash desk. "And even once they're out there, on the floor, it keeps going wrong, with all the interruptions."

I'm still babbling as I root in the drawer for the video cassette when my hand flies to my mouth, wishing I could stuff the words back in. "Oh no, I'm so sorry, I wasn't thinking and now I'm spoiling it for you."

"It's alright, we've seen it before."

"Really?" My fumbling fingers finally fit the cassette into the case.

"Yeah, no big deal," she says as I go to ring it up.

Feeling like an idiot, I ask for her membership card.

"Um," she flushes furiously, "I forgot my card but you should be able to find it on the computer."

We're not allowed to do that. The excuse dies on my lips. I've made enough of a fool of myself already. "Sure, what's your name?"

"Kit Lawless," she replies. "7 St Lawrence Place."

Kit, I mull it over to myself, wondering what it's short for. It suits her I suppose, with her dark hair and pointy face. Oh no, this is a nightmare. "Um, it's not coming up."

"Try Felice Carr!"

The name appears immediately and I look at Kit in confusion, uncertain what to do. This is exactly what Andy warned me against.

"Just let me pay for it, right?" She thrusts a five pound note at me.

I've no choice, I can't refuse. Praying Andy won't pick

this moment to come back, I count out the change and hand her the video with a weak smile. "Hope you enjoy it, again!"

"Thanks," she replies, "welcome to Drimshanra."

I watch the door long after she's gone, lost in thought. Part of me is hoping the video will be returned and I won't lose my job. It should be my main worry, but for some reason, my head is full of the girl, wondering if I'll see her again.

Kit Lawless. The name suits her, but she can't be a regular since she doesn't have a card.

Chapter 2

Andy is right about the shop getting busier later on. Harried parents come in on their way home from work, laden down with bags of shopping, desperate for something to keep the kids quiet after dinner. Between seven and eight, the teens appear. Still too young to go out, they want the perfect video for a night in with friends. The young lovers come later, looking for an excuse to curl up together on the couch. After the rush ends around eleven, Andy says he's done and asks me to close at midnight.

His request makes me uneasy but I can't afford to fall out with my boss on my first day, so I let him show me what needs to be done.

"You'll do well here," he claps me on the shoulder as he leaves. His words confirm my suspicions. He's not supposed to leave me on my own but I just nod and watch him disappear down the street.

A rowdy crowd, on the way back to someone's gaff from the pub, come in half an hour later and I wish Andy was there to help. Eventually they get what they want and leave, though I feel a bit shaky after they are gone. Then a few stragglers come in just before midnight. Andy would probably state firmly that we were closed, but he's not here. Without his authority, I don't like to turn them away. By the time I finally lock the door behind me, it's close to one in the morning.

I can't help wondering if that's why my boss was so anxious to get away early, especially since this is pretty much the exact same time the pubs in Drimshanra empty out into the streets. With a shiver, I button up my navy reefer and pull the collar up around my ears. It's not just to keep out the cold drizzle, but to blend into the night. An odour of urine and vomit oozes from darkened doorways and you can feel the pulse of danger flicker in the air.

Ahead of me, two young guys are thrown from a bar in a tangle of limbs.

"I'll get you yet, you two ends of a knob." One of them hauls himself to his feet and shakes his fist at the bouncer.

"Yeah." The other crawls out of the gutter.

"Fuck off, Sledge," the bouncer replies, "and don't let me catch you with any of your underage friends in here again."

It's too late to cross the street, it would only draw attention to myself. I put my head down and quicken my pace, hoping Sledge and his pal don't notice me. Main Street is too busy, too bright, with nowhere to hide. By taking the short cut, I can melt into the shadows, and pass unnoticed in the dark. I hunch my shoulders tighter into my coat and quicken my step. Leaving Main Street is a mistake. The real danger lingers in dark alleys like this one.

"The gay bar!" I hear a shout behind me and press myself in against the metal shutter of a closed shop, as Sledge barrels by.

"Yeah, get the poofters." His friend is hot on his heels.

The two disappear out of sight around the corner and I exhale with relief. My route home is the same way they've gone, but I follow at a slow pace, giving them plenty of time to get ahead of me.

The back streets aren't as quiet as I expect. Instead, they are lined with the kind of places that come alive at night but are invisible when the shutters are down during the day. The gay bar must be somewhere along here. I wonder if Sledge and his friend will get in and what kind of havoc they'll wreak if they do.

As I walk on up the street, the Saturday night revels fade into the distance behind me. Home is close now, just around the corner, and, thankfully, there's no sign of Sledge or his friend. They must have found somewhere to go after all.

My body is trembling and I can't wait to get inside the house and bolt the door behind me. It's funny, I didn't expect Drimshanra to have this effect on me, not after the estate we lived on in Dublin, but it's like something evil and malevolent is lurking in the shadows here.

As I round the final corner, I hear a scuffle and faint shouts in the distance, the distinct sound of feet running away, boots pounding the pavement. Sledge and his friend. It has to be. Gone.

Something moves at the end of the street, catching my eye. A heap of black, like a plastic sack, burst and spewing out its contents. Except as I draw closer, I see it's not a black plastic sack. It's a person curled up in agony, with blood pooling on the street around him.

I try not to look, try not to step in it.

Want to avoid the whole thing.

It's been a long day and I wish it was over.

So close to home, almost in bed, where I can pull the covers over my head and pretend the assault didn't happen, the way I used to when Dad was still around.

The figure shifts slightly and lets out a low moan.

It's no good, I'm not seven years old any more.

I can't ignore this one.

"Wait there," I say, not that he looks capable of going anywhere, "I'll be right back."

The house is just a few doors down, and I silently let myself in so as not to wake my mother. I lift the receiver of the phone in the cramped hallway, dial 999, and ask for an ambulance.

Then I dash into my room, whisk the duvet off my bed and sprint back outside. It's still raining, not heavily, just a damp persistent drizzle that chills to the core. I hope he's still alive as I cover him up as best I can. Shivering, my teeth chattering, I sit on the kerb beside him and wait for the ambulance.

"You did well to cover him up," a burly paramedic says as they lift him onto the stretcher. "They made some mess of him but I don't think anything is broken. Maybe a cracked rib."

But I'm not listening. For the first time, I can see the boy's face through the matted hair and streaks of blood. He's young, about my age, and he looks so pale and vulnerable. Why would anyone pick on him in such a brutal way?

"Do you know him?"

I shake my head.

"Did you see what happened?" the paramedic asks me then.

"No, not exactly."

"You'd better come with us."

I climb into the ambulance beside the stretcher.

Under the paramedics' care, the boy starts to come round.

"Spike O'Toole, nice to see you back with us. Who did it this time?"

Spike ignores the question and turned to me

"My rescuer?" His voice is cracked and dry. He holds out his hand, and when I take it, he doesn't let go. "Stay with me," he murmurs.

"So who did it this time?" The paramedic asks again. My stomach contracts as it dawns on me that he knows Spike, that this has happened before.

"Came up on me from behind, didn't see a thing."

"And I suppose you didn't see him when he hit your face either?"

"No, couldn't focus too well."

"What about you?" The paramedic turns to me. "Did you see anything?"

"Not exactly but…" Spike's grip tightens in warning. The message is clear. He doesn't want me to say anything.

"But what?" the paramedic presses for an answer

"But I was too far away. I heard someone run away."

The guards are waiting at the hospital but Spike and I stick to our story. Neither of us saw anything.

"Not much we can do without witnesses," the guards grumble as Spike is wheeled off for an x-ray. As they turn to leave, one of them says to me, "You can go home now if you want."

"It's alright, I'll wait and see how he is." Now that I'm involved, I feel like I have to stay and see the whole thing through. Sitting on a plastic chair in the corridor, I doze off, losing track of time. Eventually, Spike is wheeled out again and brought into a curtained-off cubicle in the overcrowded Accident and Emergency Unit. Once again I get a sense of a malevolent presence that poisons the air in Drimshanra.

"Nothing is broken," the nurse tells me, "so he doesn't

need to be kept in."

"Really?" I stare in surprise at the barely conscious bandaged body in the bed.

"It looks worse than it is," she says. "Can you take him home?"

"I mean, I don't really know...," I start to say.

Spike interrupts me by reaching for my hand. He tries to clutch it, but his grip is too weak and his fingers fall loosely to his side. "Can you call someone to come and get me?" he asks in a hoarse whisper.

"Sure, who do you want me to call?"

"Felice Carr."

Chapter 3

The name surprises me because I recognise it immediately. It's the name Kit Lawless got me to look up at work. Spike murmurs the number to me and I jot it down.

There's a pay phone halfway down the corridor, and I push in some coins and dial the number.

"Yeah?" a girl with a bored London accent answers.

"Is that Felice Carr?"

"Why?" Her tone changes abruptly. "Who is this?"

I explain about Spike being attacked and tell her he's in hospital looking for her.

"Jesus, yeah, sure. Tell him we'll be right there."

When I get back into the cubicle, the nurse sticks her head through the curtain. Once she hears Spike's friends are coming to get him, she nods satisfied.

"Will you wait with me till they get here?" Spike croaks.

"Sure!" There's a chair beside his trolley and I do my best to make myself comfortable.

Spike can barely speak so we wait in silence. Even though it's getting close to 3 am and it's been a long, tiring day, I feel wide awake. Perhaps it's nervous energy. My mind is full of questions. This isn't the first time he's been assaulted, so why won't Spike report the attack?

It makes no sense, especially when the guards encouraged him to do so. One thing I have figured out is that Spike is eighteen, like me. Since he's no longer a minor, the guards don't need his parents present to speak to him and the hospital doesn't have to contact them either.

Felice Carr, who is she? Perhaps she's his girlfriend, but for some reason, that doesn't feel right. It's hard to say why exactly. Maybe it was the tone of exasperation in her voice, on the phone. Still, I'm a little jealous. If it was me in Spike's position, I'd be looking for my mother, because I don't have anybody else. It's not just that I'm new here. There wasn't anyone where I lived before either.

And then a happier thought strikes me. If Spike knows Felice, it's possible he knows Kit too, which means I might meet her again. For the first time, I'm almost glad I'm the one who found him and came to the hospital with him.

The clamour and din of Accident and Emergency is settling down after a busy Saturday night when the air shifts.

Boots clatter down the corridor and a bored English drawl vibrates through the space. "Where is he this time? I've got a bag of stuff for him."

"He won't be needing it," a nurse replies, "the doctor has seen him and he's not being admitted. He's over there, if you want to take him home."

A moment later the curtain of the cubicle is yanked back. Two girls rush in and lean over the bed, gasping with horror as they survey the injured occupant.

"They went for my face," Spike murmurs, his voice weak and strained.

"He shouldn't be speaking." Neither of them noticed me in the corner and they both freeze at the sound of my voice.

"Sorry, I didn't mean to startle you." I stand up and look straight at the second girl, the one I recognised instantly.

Kit Lawless.

"Hey, nothing scares us!" Felice tosses her eye-catching

blue hair.

"I'm Tully. Tully Cabe."

Together, the girls make an intimidating pair as they stare at me, waiting to hear what happened. In make-up and a leather jacket, Kit looks older than she did earlier.

It's not easy telling the girls how their friend was beaten up and left lying on the street. I stumble a few times, getting caught up in explanations, but neither of them are as shocked as I expect.

"Well, thanks for looking out for him," Felice says when I get to the end.

"It was no trouble." Feeling awkward, I turn to Kit. "I saw you earlier, didn't I? You rented Strictly Ballroom."

"Jesus, don't tell me you paid for it?" Felice rounds on her friend, like that's a more serious offence than Spike's injuries.

"Felice is your boss's daughter," Kit explains, rolling her eyes.

"What, Andy has a daughter?" With her blue hair and heavy eyeliner, Felice must be at least seventeen. There's no way Andy is old enough to be her father.

Felice snorts with laughter.

"I guess you haven't met my dad," she says. "Andy's the manager. Dad owns the whole chain."

"Your dad is Axel Carr?" Of course, Felice Carr! I feel like an idiot for not making the connection till now. More Video 4U is all over the country, in every town in Ireland, but I'd no idea Drimshanra was Axel Carr's home territory.

"Yeah," Felice's tone is menacing, "me and my friends always get our videos for free."

"I'm really sorry." Shit, this is bad. I can't afford to get on the wrong side of the boss's daughter on my first day. I'm still on trial and Felice with her studs and spiky jewellery oozes confrontation. "I didn't know."

"It's not his fault," Kit says, "I didn't tell him."

It's nice of her to stand up for me, but now Felice glares at her friend. "Kit, how many times do we have to go through this? You have to tell the new staff, okay?"

"Got it." Kit sends me a conspiratorial look.

"So, can we leave now?" Spike rasps from the bed.

"The nurse said he can go." Felice turns from me to Kit and shrugs.

"Come on," Spike pleads, "take me back to yours."

He's in no shape to go anywhere except straight home to bed. Yet despite Felice's militant attitude, there is a dynamic between the three of them. The bond that binds them together is so strong, I can almost touch it. None of them would ever let either of the others down. At least that's how it feels to me. Not for the first time, I envy Kit Lawless.

"Alright!" Felice finally breaks the silence and the tension eases. "Let's get you out of here!"

The next few minutes are spent with a nurse who organises a taxi and makes sure Spike has a supply of painkillers to get him through the night. As I watch him being heaved off the trolley into a wheelchair, I can't help wondering if Felice is the best person to look after him. Still, Kit is there too and Spike looks a lot more cheerful now he's leaving A&E. By the time we get down to the exit, the taxi has arrived. Kit fusses over him as he's carefully loaded into it. As Felice takes off her oversized coat and hands it to Kit to cover the invalid, I catch a glimpse of a tattoo peeking out under the low waist of her shiny tracksuit bottoms

"You did good," she says to me.

"No problem, I wasn't doing anything else. I don't know anyone here yet."

"Hey, you know us now," she replies with a smile and climbs into the passenger seat.

Kit doesn't wave from behind the window as the taxi pulls away. My final glimpse is of her profile staring straight ahead. If I didn't know better, I'd almost think she was ignoring me.

Chapter 4

Feeling a little deflated, I make my way home through the silent, deserted streets, keeping my head down against the persistent drizzle. The mist conceals me but there's no longer anything to hide from. Several hours have passed and even the most dedicated revellers and trouble-makers have disappeared behind closed doors.

The image of the taxi disappearing into the night stays with me, Spike cocooned in its warm, comfortable security, his friends around him. I wonder where Axel Carr's house is and what it's like. In my imagination, it's a palatial old pile with immense grounds, hidden away in some discreet corner of the town.

I reach our house and fumble for my key. The paint on the door is peeling and it looks as dingy as you'd expect of a low-rent property in a dead end town. We've always lived in places like this, crappy lodgings that Mam struggles to afford. My dream is to buy her a house of her own one day, not a huge mansion like Axel Carr's, just somewhere small she can call her own and where she won't have to worry about how to pay the rent every month.

That's why the job in More Video 4U is so important to us. Right now, we're both depending on my wage because Mam hasn't found work yet. She hasn't been well since the move and though she insists it's nothing, I can't help being worried.

It's hard to get to sleep, but I drift off in the end, and wake up to the sun streaming in through the windows. The smell of frying bacon fills the tiny house, filtering in under my bedroom door, reminding me how hungry I am. I never got a chance to eat properly yesterday.

"Did you get in very late last night?" Mam asks when I burst into the kitchen, "I wanted to wait up but I must have fallen asleep." She throws a sausage onto the pan and tells me to make toast.

It's already eleven o'clock but, luckily, I'm on the afternoon shift. As I wolf my mother's breakfast down, I summarise the events of the night, downplaying Spike's injuries because I don't want to alarm her.

"You're a hero!" She comes up behind my chair and puts her arms around me. If anything happened to me, Mam wouldn't hesitate. She'd drop everything and fly to my rescue. I can't help wondering, yet again, why Spike wanted Kit and Felice instead of his family. "I'm glad you've made some new friends."

That's the thing though, I'm not sure I have. Kit, Felice and Spike live in a completely different world to mine. There's no reason to think I'll see any of them again unless they come into the shop.

The afternoon at work stretches to infinity. Every time the shop bell pings, I look up in anticipation in case Kit walks through the door. Every time the phone rings behind the counter, I think it might be one of them, with an update on Spike's progress. But the day wears on, Kit doesn't come in and the phone is never for me.

The next day I take the longer route to work, past her front door. I'm both hoping for a glimpse of her, and nervous in case she sees me and thinks I'm stalking her. The day is bright and the sun sparkles on the Georgian window panes. In the rain the other day, I didn't notice a steep flight of steps leading down to a separate entrance in the basement of the house.

A sign on the railing in front of it reads 'Lawless and Sons, Solicitors' in an elegant and discreet script.

With her leather jacket, red lipstick and friends like Felice and Spike, Kit is not exactly the daughter you'd expect Mr Lawless of Lawless & Sons, Solicitors, to have, but it makes no difference. Her family is well-off and well-educated, there's no reason she'd ever look at me. It's a depressing reminder that I've nothing to offer her.

As the days drag by, a part of me is constantly waiting for one of them to darken the door. There are often moments when I'm tempted to tell Andy abut meeting Felice Carr, and ask him what he knows about her and her friends. But something holds me back.

It's an instinct that the only way to discover who they really are is by getting to know them in person, not through rumour or hearsay. Somehow it seems disloyal to gossip about them. But I don't even know why I feel that, because they've clearly forgotten all about me.

It's like they've disappeared or were a figment of my imagination. In one day I saw Kit Lawless three times. It was as though I couldn't stop running into her and now she's vanished off the face of the earth.

Andy is waiting to hand over when I arrive in after lunch on Friday. "You'll be alright on your own tonight?"

he asks, "it will be busy."

"No problem." I don't like to remind him he left me by myself last Friday and that was my first day.

"Well, you have my number just in case," Andy says, "but you've been doing well, so I'm sure you'll be fine. Bet you're looking forward to a couple of days off?"

Truth is I'd rather work. There's nothing else to do and we need the money.

I'm just about to tell Andy this when he slaps his head. "Hey, I almost forgot, someone rang for you earlier. Here, I took a message." He passes me a scrap of paper which I scan eagerly.

Spike called. They are all going to the Black Death gig in Fibber's tomorrow and you're welcome to join them.

"Do you know anything about this?" I ask Andy. He goes in to be a music buff and has the radio constantly playing in the shop.

"Yeah, Black Death, they're doing really well at the moment. You must have heard their song, Plagued By You, on the radio? It's flying up the charts. The singer, Mac Whitehead, has this amazing voice, really distinctive. All the girls are mad about him and everyone's saying they're the next big thing."

"Oh yeah," I've heard the song and Andy is right

about Mac Whitehead's throaty vocals, "so they're local, are they?"

"Nah, think they're from Dublin. Surprised they're playing in a dump like Fibber's though. I suppose the gig must have been booked before their single started to do well. They should be getting bigger venues now."

"Yeah, makes sense," I murmur, not remotely interested in Black Death, but ecstatic because Spike's message has changed everything.

Suddenly I'm thrilled to have Saturday off, because now I have somewhere to go and people to meet. It feels like the stars are aligned and everything is falling into place. Drimshanra is transformed from a grey and dreary nowhere town into an exciting destination, abounding with promise and possibility.

I read the note again. They're all going… That means Kit will be there. Finally, I'll get to see her again. There have been moments when I felt there was a connection, like when she welcomed me to Drimshanra, like when she defended me to Felice. But there have been others when I've wondered if I'm annoying her, or whether she even wants to talk to me, like when she didn't say goodbye at the hospital, like the way there hasn't been a word from her since.

A small voice at the back of my head warns me not to get too excited, not to raise my hopes up too high, that perhaps it's all in my head, but I don't listen. Kit and her friends are by far the most interesting thing about Drimshanra.

They are what makes it come alive.

Without them, it's dead.

Chapter 5

My wardrobe is basic, which suits me. I've never tried to stand out because usually I'm happy to blend in. But now that I want something to wear for the concert tonight, my cupboard is bare. Just thinking of Kit and her friends makes me wish I could buy something new. The problem is I haven't been paid yet.

"Off to meet your new friends?" Mam asks with a twinkle in her eye when she sees me ironing my one and only white shirt.

"Yeah, we're going to a gig in town." It feels good saying 'we'.

"To think I was worried about how you'd get on here in Drimshanra. It's nothing like Dublin, but you're doing so well. You've got a job and made new friends already."

The shirt is warm from the iron and I smile as I button it up.

"You look so handsome," she says admiringly. She's biased because she's my mother, although she was beautiful once, and people say I take after her. My hair is lighter than hers, and curlier, but we have the same brown eyes. Mam used to have long black hair, dark and lustrous, but now it's streaked with grey and falls untidily around her shoulders. She's thin and fragile as a bird as I stoop to kiss her goodbye.

The summer evenings are long and it's still light as I head out into the night's warm embrace, buzzing with anticipation. I know what Mam means about Dublin, but though most people wouldn't agree with me, I think there are more opportunities in Drimshanra. I never met anyone like Kit or Felice when I was in Dublin.

Our area had a bad name and nobody with money lived there. The school was the same. The teachers did their best but nobody wanted to be there. Everyone knew the future was on the streets, working for the gangs. Most kids didn't mind. It's what you do if you grow up in dodgy parts of town and it has a kind of glamour to it – exciting, dangerous and well-paid if short-lived.

It never appealed to me. All I've ever wanted, ever

dreamed of for me and Mam, is a normal life, simple with no drama, the kind of life I've never had.

Fibber's is one of those closed up venues that's invisible by day but once the shutters roll up at night, the place comes alive. There's already a queue down the street when I arrive but there's no sign of the three friends. As I wait in line, I wonder if I should have come earlier. Suppose, it's sold out and I can't get in?

The place is heaving by the time I finally make it through the door. The light is so dim, I start to panic. Suppose they're not here? Or they are here, but I can't find them in the dark?

Then I spot a flash of blue hair in the middle of the crowd, and push my way towards it before it disappears.

"Hey, Tully, over here!" Spike catches sight of me and waves. He's fearless in a purple tie and pointed boots, with his shaggy Goth hair and kohl-rimmed eyes.

"You look much better." The only trace of last week's injuries are the dark circles around his eyes. If you didn't know otherwise, the bruises could pass for make-up in the shadowy light.

"Why didn't you report them?" I ask the question that's been burning on my mind ever since.

"I can't." He pulls me in close and murmurs in my ear.

"I haven't come out to my family yet."

"Oh." Suddenly, everything falls into place and it all makes sense. That's why he didn't tell the guards anything, why he wanted Felice and Kit instead of his family. I feel so stupid. I don't know how I didn't see it before.

"Don't worry," I mutter back, "I won't say anything."

"I didn't think you would." His smile is amused.

The three of them stand out like exotic birds, Felice at the front of the pack, bright and vivid, impossible to miss with her pastel hair, Kit more discreet and understated in black. She's wearing a black lace top that shows off her curves and self-confidence. Together, they are untouchable, invincible. Some drunken idiots might pick on Spike alone, in a dark alley, but they won't go near him here, not when the three of them are together. Looking at them, I'm relieved I didn't have any money to spend on clothes. Anything I could have bought in Drimshanra would have been all wrong.

"Hey," Kit mumbles without looking at me.

"Hey," Felice links her arm through mine and elbows her way through the crowd, right up to the very front.

We arrive just as the band leaps out onto the stage, almost on top of us. The whole place goes wild, the crowd a sweaty seething mass around us. I'd rather stay at the back, where I might get a chance to talk to Kit, but I should have guessed Felice would only be happy jammed up against the stage in the middle of the action.

Andy was right about the girls loving Mac Whitehead. Kit is misty-eyed and can't take her eyes off him and she's not the only one. Bare-chested, in ripped jeans, he glides around the stage like he owns it.

There's no option but to join in, so I shout and pump my arms like the best of them. To be fair, Mac Whitehead has a compelling stage presence, and I find myself pulled into the music and caught under his spell. Whatever Mac sings, the crowd are happy to listen and cheer long. When the band plays 'Plagued by You', the song that's rocketing up the charts, the crowd go wild, shouting the chorus back at him at the tops of their voices.

When the set is finally over, the crowd keeps asking for more and the band plays several encores. Eventually, it really is over. The lights go on, revealing the drab interior and littered floor, and the place starts to empty out. Spike wanders off but, thankfully, Kit and Felice don't seem in any rush to leave. Instead they hover around hopefully.

"That was amazing," I make my voice sound as

enthusiastic as possible, because I know it's the right thing to say.

"Have you seen them before?" Felice asks.

"Never. Don't know much about them, except that song on the radio."

"Plagued by You." Felice has a sceptical look in her eyes that tells me she's not buying it, but Kit gives me a tiny, supportive smile that makes my heart race.

"Guys, you won't believe this," Spike rushes up to us, stuttering with excitement, "I know the sound guy. They need a hand loading up the gear. C'mon, we'll get to meet the band."

"No way!" As one we race out of the building after Spike. He leads us to an alley at the back, where the band has parked the van.

I can't believe my luck. I was hoping something would happen to make the night last longer and give me a chance to chat to Kit. This is the perfect opportunity. Jumping into the back of the van, I take a box from the guitarist. He tells me his name is Baz and introduces his girlfriend, Jenna. Kit drifts over and starts chatting to Jenna, watching us idly. Felice is flirting with the drummer and neither of them are doing anything to help.

It's only when Felice asks where Mac Whitehead is

that I notice the lead singer's absence.

"At the bar, chatting up the girls," Jenna rolls her eyes, "as usual."

Kit looks away and I can tell she's trying to hide her disappointment but, inwardly, I'm jubilant. Without him to distract her, there's a better chance she'll talk to me.

"It's hard for Mac to get away," Baz says. "They all want a piece of him."

"The rest of you manage it," Jenna says with asperity and I hide a grin. Some girls can resist Mac's charms.

As the night goes on, we get a rhythm going. Baz passes the boxes and I stack them, while Spike helps the sound guy carry the stuff out to us. The four of us, Baz, Jenna, Kit and I chat away as we load the van. There's still no sign of Mac, but the longer he stays away, the happier I am. The time passes quickly. Baz tells us stories about the band and how the success of 'Plagued by You' has turned them into a big deal and a hot new act. Black Death is definitely going places. An hour later it's all done and we no longer have an excuse to hang around.

"Thanks for helping out," Baz says.

"No problem," I reply. "Great to meet you all!" Not that there's any chance we'll meet again. There's no reason for an up and coming band to hang around

Drimshanra, not when they have so many bigger, brighter places to go. Still, I can't help noticing when Len, the drummer Felice has been flirting with all night, writes down his number and hands it to her.

The three friends head towards the main street to hunt down a taxi. Once again, I find myself walking home alone. But this time is different. Even though nothing has been said, I feel sure I'll see them again.

Chapter 6

By this stage, I'm getting used to the routine in More Video 4U and the second week passes quickly. Andy schedules me to work most shifts on my own, which I take as a good sign. Some of the regulars have started to recognise me and sometimes stop and chat for a bit when they come into the shop. Once again, there's no sign of Kit or her friends, but I'm not worried. Sooner or later, one of them will get in touch.

Sure enough, on Thursday afternoon, Felice drops in during the quiet time. While she's browsing the latest arrivals, she suddenly says, "Do you want to come to a party on Saturday?"

"Sure," I reply, "at your place?"

"Not exactly, Black Death has decided to spend the summer in Drimshanra."

"Really?" I can't keep the surprise out of my voice.

"Yeah, really, what's so amazing about that? They have to live somewhere. Do you want to come to the house-warming or not?"

"Sure!"

As she scribbles down the address, I'm dying to ask her more, like why on earth a hot new act would think it was a good idea to move to Drimshanra, but her glare puts me off.

"Okay, I'm taking all of these." She dumps a pile of videos on the counter in front of me and I fill the empty sleeves.

She grins when I don't try to ring it up. Inwardly, I've made a mental note of the films and I'll ask Andy what to do when I see him.

"See you Saturday," she says.

"Can't wait," I reply, but she's already gone.

Andy arrives in the evening and I tell him about Felice's visit to the shop.

"Yeah, just as well you didn't try to ring it up. People have been fired for less."

"You can't be serious?" Feeling grateful to Kit for the warning, I swallow a gulp. I'd begun to think Felice was all bark and no bite.

"Oh yeah, she's a wild cat, that one! But she's the boss's daughter and there's nothing we can do about it. Just bring up her file and make a note of anything she borrows. At least that way we can track the inventory."

"And supposing she doesn't bring them back on time?"

"Bring them back on time?" Andy almost screeches. "She never brings them back on time. We're lucky if she brings them back at all. Anyway," he resumes in a calmer tone, "you've been here two weeks, more or less, so your trial is over! The job is yours if you want it."

Of course I want it. It's such a relief I almost hug him. "That's great, thanks so much."

"Yeah, so make the most of this weekend. Starting Monday, it's going to be full time, lots of Saturday nights. I don't want you letting me down."

"Yes, boss, I'm yours to command," I snap my heels together with a mock salute.

"Sometimes I wonder where we got you from." He's smiling as he shakes his head.

"Hey, Andy, do you know where this is?" I show him the address Felice gave me.

"Yeah, it's that new estate the other side of town, out the Dublin Road. You'll need a car to get there."

I nod, satisfied. Mam will lend me hers.

Mam and I spend Saturday morning unpacking the last remaining boxes. There's only a couple left, with nothing much in them, a few ornaments from second-hand shops and my old school-books. Those might as well stay in the box as far as I'm concerned but, while there's no attic in the tiny house, there is an alcove beside the miniature fireplace in the living room. Mam is anxious to find stuff to fill the shelves built into it. Perhaps she thinks it will make the place look more cheerful and homely, but the random selection of text books and old-fashioned china just looks odd.

"Hmm, it still needs something," she says, "perhaps some new curtains? Let's have a cup of tea and think about it."

When I've put on the kettle, I ask if I can borrow her car.

"Of course, it's wonderful the way you have a social life already. But you'll remember not to drink?"

"I won't drink, Mam," I say softly. Even though we never talk about him, we both remember Dad. Let's just say alcohol has zero appeal for me. Mam knows that perfectly well.

"It's great you've got the job." She runs her hand through my hair.

"It's a big chain. Over time I might get promoted."

"I'm sure you will," her smile is a little forlorn, "they're lucky to have you. And so am I. Now I need to hurry up and get a job too."

"There's no rush, Mam. We're still only getting settled in." I was hoping getting out of the city would be good for her, but she's as pale as ever and, if anything, the circles under her eyes are darker. "It's a nice day, do you want to go for a drive, see some of the countryside? Maybe we could get lunch somewhere, to celebrate my new job, now it's official?"

"That's a lovely idea," she gives me a quick hug, "but let's wait till things are a bit more stable and we've some money in the kitty."

She's right of course. Moving is an expensive business, with all kinds of extras you don't think of, like the way the landlord always finds some reason to keep most of your deposit when you leave a place, but you still have to pay the full deposit on the next one. Then there was the van we rented to move all our stuff, and a few things we needed to replace when we got here. Besides, even though I have a job, I won't be paid till the end of the month, so things are especially tight at the moment. Still, I'm sorry we can't get out of this dank and gloomy house.

I spend the afternoon upstairs in my room, listening to music and practising guitar, imagining I'm playing for Kit. I decide to wear the Nirvana t-shirt Mam gave me for my birthday to the party. I hardly ever wear it because I don't want it to go from velvety black to washed-out grey, but I'm hoping tonight it will bring me luck.

"Don't wait up for me, Mam," I say when I'm leaving. "I don't know what time the party ends."

"You stay as long as you like. And don't worry about me. I'm going to have an early night."

Are you sure you're alright? The question hovers on my lips but something in her expression stops me from asking it aloud. It's unspoken between us, the agreement that Mam isn't ill. I just wish I still believed it.

"Go, enjoy yourself! You need to get out, mix with people your own age!" She shoos me playfully out the door. I love her when she's like this, vivacious and teasing, instead of pretending not to be in pain.

The big new estate is easy enough to find, though the house itself is more of a challenge. It's nicer than the last place we lived in Dublin. The houses are bigger and smarter, but I can't help wondering what it will be like in twenty years time. Will it live up to the promise of the advertisements, with prosperous families strolling around with prams and a new car in the driveway, or will it have deteriorated? Will it be like my former home, windblown tracts, with rubbish and broken glass, shadowy figures lurking at corners, residents hiding inside once it gets dark, a couple of abandoned, burnt-out lots where kids hang out getting drunk and high? Houses grown shabby because there's no money to maintain them, tiny front gardens overgrown with weeds and piled high with junk, a hopeless air of misery hanging over the place. It could have been worse. At least by that point I'd learned to become invisible. It's the only way to survive in a place like that. Nobody picked on me, I was just an anonymous teenager everyone ignored.

My mood lifts as I turn a corner and see a brightly lit house straight ahead, a crowd of young people gathered on the cobble locked driveway and music blaring through the open front door. I park at the kerb and walk up the street, buoyed up by a sense of optimism as I approach the cheery scene, golden in the late evening light.

The dreary estate on the outskirts of the city is in the past. Who knows, this house in Drimshanra might hold the key to my future. It's a strange thought and I don't know why it comes into my head, but the truth is I feel like my destiny is about to unfold.

At first I thought it was just the relief of being somewhere new, but now I'm beginning to believe that Drimshanra is the fresh start I've always dreamed of, the one where I can re-invent myself.

Perhaps this time, I can actually be somebody.

Chapter 7

It takes a moment to find a familiar face in the crowd milling around outside, but then I spot Spike and go over to him.

"Good man, Tully, you made it," he says. "Felice is over there somewhere stuck to Len." He waves towards the far corner of the house. "I'd leave them alone if I was you. Kit was inside last time I saw her, in the living room."

"I'll go look for her!" Spike is by far the friendliest and most welcoming of the friends, but Kit's the one I really want to find.

"You do that." There's a knowing gleam in his eye that I take as a sign of encouragement.

The sitting room is dominated by a huge couch, draped with the kind of colourful throw you can get at an

Indian market stall. Mac Whitehead sits in the middle of it, a couple of girls either side. The curtains at the bay window behind the couch have been left open and I spot Kit, smoking a cigarette, almost hidden behind one of them.

"I wonder where Baz and Jenna are?" I say when I've greeted her.

"I haven't seen them yet." She shoves up to make room on the window ledge beside her and watches as I take a sip from the can of coke. "Not drinking?"

"Can't, I'm driving."

"Really? How old are you?"

"Eighteen." I'm not sure whether to be flattered or insulted by the look of surprise she throws at me. "And you?"

"Seventeen."

"You're still in school?"

"Yeah, what about you? Did you do exams this year? Where do you want to go to college?" It's the first time Kit has shown any interest in talking to me, but her questions aren't the kind I find easy to answer.

"I've no plans like that. There's no chance of me going to college. I quit school when I was sixteen." It comes out sounding abrupt, which isn't what I intended, but she's touched a nerve. I'm not like Kit and her friends, with every opportunity thrown at me.

"Really?" She sounds more interested than shocked. "Why?"

"I didn't like it," I shrug. "I couldn't wait to get out of there, to be honest. You can leave once you're sixteen, you know that, right?" Thankfully, school is behind me now and it's not something I want to dwell on. For me, it's all about moving forward.

But Kit's not ready to let it go yet. "What about your parents?" she asks. "What did they think?"

"There's only me and Mam. My dad split years ago." I wait for the disapproval to register on her face.

"Bet everyone blamed your mother," she surprises me by saying, "though it was probably your dad's fault."

I stare at her in amazement. "How did you know?"

"Felice's parents are divorced," she says, "and Felice blames her dad."

"I didn't know Axel Carr was divorced."

"Andy's such a gossip I'm surprised he didn't tell you, but I suppose it's old news. They got divorced years ago."

"How did they manage that?" I ask. Divorce has only recently become legal in Ireland. Up till then, my parents' separation was an on-going scandal.

"They didn't get married in Ireland. Felice's mum is English. She lives in London now."

So that explains the English accent and avant-garde wardrobe. "It must be hard on Felice, not having her mum around."

"I guess," Kit shrugs and looks around. I'm not sure if it's because she doesn't want to discuss Felice's business with me, which is fair enough, or because she's tired of talking to me.

I try to win her back with a topic that seemed to interest her. "You're right though, Mam was disappointed when I quit school. I kind of feel like I've let her down. She gave up a lot for me. She wanted more for me than working in More Video 4U."

"But you won't be doing that for the rest of your life!" Kit warms up again.

"I hope not, but I don't exactly have any qualifications. What about you? What are you going to do?"

"Law."

"Law? Wow, you must be really brainy." Law is really hard to get into. Even I know that, and Kit doesn't strike me as an academic.

"I'm being forced into it. My dad wants me to take over the family practice."

"That's cool. It gives you a direction. At least you know where you're going. I've no clue where my life will lead." She's no idea how lucky she is. She doesn't need to worry about anything. It's all being handed to her on a plate.

"Yes," she says, "but I feel like I've no choice. I'd rather have the freedom to pick my own future."

"And what would you choose if you could?"

"I don't know. What about you, what would you choose?"

"Me? Music. I want to be in a band, like him," I nod over at Mac Whitehead, enthroned on the couch. "I'm a walking cliché, no wonder my poor mother's almost given up on me."

"You like blondes?"

"What? No. You think I want the groupies?" We both watch as Mac takes a girl by the hand and leads her out of the room, but that's not what I meant at all, and I'm mortified she thinks I did. "No, for me it's about the music. It's all about the music, just that and nothing else."

"I'm going to get a drink," she says, getting up.

And I wonder what went wrong. It seemed to be going well, but I lost her at music. How could that be when she seems so into it? It hits me like a blow to my stomach –

Mac Whitehead and the way she looked at him.

But no, that can't be it.

Surely she can tell he's no interest in her.

Even if he had, it wouldn't last. Mac's just in it for a good time, but maybe that's something girls can't see.

Still, if Kit fancies Mac Whitehead there's no way she'll look at me.

Why would she? What have I got to offer?

The party is flat after she's gone, and I'm thinking I might as well leave when Felice catches hold of me.

"Hey Tully!"

"Yeah?"

"Kit says you drove here."

"That's right."

"Any chance you could give us a lift back to my place?"

She's the boss's daughter so it's not like I can say no. Besides it strikes me she's had a lot to drink and mightn't be too clear what she's asking.

"Sure, no problem!"

That's how I end up driving out through the dark countryside in the middle of the night. Spike is beside me in the front seat with Kit, Felice and Len squashed into the back of my mother's tiny grey Honda.

"I thought Felice lived in town," I say to Spike.

"No, why would you think that?"

"I guess I just assumed."

Spike looks through my mother's tape collection and picks a David Bowie album which he shoves in the deck. "This yours?" he asks as the opening riff of 'The Man Who Saved the World' breaks the silence in the car.

"Mam's."

"She has good taste."

"Yes," I say with a smile, "though I prefer Kurt Cobain's version."

"Yes, I suppose you would." Spike replies with a sideways glance at the Nirvana logo scrolled across my chest. He settles back into his seat and the poignant lyrics fill the car as we travel down narrow twisty roads. It seems so far from the estate where the party was, like another world.

Urban spaces have rules and you can figure them out and find a way to fit in, but by night, the country is wild and chaotic, subject to the whims of nature, forces beyond our control.

The headlights cut swathes through the darkness, revealing glimpses of overgrown hedges and limbs of trees, distorted by shadows. Under the night sky, the endless turns in the road have a dreamlike quality, as though time has no meaning. I don't know what strange mood is on me but I feel as though we've been driving all night and are lost, on a road to nowhere. Yet we haven't even listened to the first side of the tape when Spike tells me to turn in at the next entrance.

In the dark, I almost overshoot it. Carefully, I steer down a long narrow lane, which takes us far off the road, deep into night. Eventually we come around a bend and a vista opens up in front of us as the twisting trail merges with a gravelled expanse leading to the house.

Instead of the historic mansion I'd imagined, a modern masterpiece rises in front of us, all sharp angles with slanted roofs and huge expanses of glass.

"Wow!" Axel Carr's ultra-contemporary architectural creation is the last thing I expected in this desolate location.

"Home, sweet home," Felice slurs. The bitterness in her voice is unmistakeable.

Chapter 8

We follow Felice through a large double-height entrance hall into an enormous living room. An over-sized L-shaped leather couch with a conveniently placed coffee-table is angled towards the largest television set I've ever seen. Everything is expensive and the couch is designed for comfort as much as aesthetics, but the huge picture windows make me uneasy. There are no curtains and the wide expanse of glass looks out into the impenetrable darkness beyond. There's something eerie about it, a disturbing sense that we are all on view, like characters on a stage, in a brightly lit set. Anything could be out there looking in, and we would never know.

The tense atmosphere seems to affect us all. Before long, everyone is making excuses to go to bed. With a shiver, I realise I'm stuck in Axel Carr's house for the night. There's no way I can find my way back to Drimshanra in the dark. Perhaps I could use the phone to let Mam know I won't be home till morning, but she promised not to wait up and there's no point in waking her at 2.00 am.

Felice takes us all upstairs and leads me to a spare room. "You can sleep here. There's a bathroom through there." She points at a door in the far wall.

The room has its own balcony and as soon as Felice has gone, I rush to draw the curtains across the French window leading out onto it. Once the darkness is closed out, I take a deep breath and look around me. Fancy isn't the right word, because there is nothing ornate about the room. But even though it's simple and understated, you can tell the pale colours and subtle details have been chosen by an interior designer. It's like something straight out of a five star hotel, not that I've ever been in a luxury hotel, or slept in a room like this before. Despite my restless agitation, I fall asleep quickly. It must be the mattress on the bed. I've never slept on anything so comfortable.

In the morning I almost don't want to get up. For an instant, I'd rather just lie there, luxuriating in the smoothness of the sheets, wondering how on earth I got here.

With a shock, I remember I'm in Axel Carr's house and Mam has no idea. She'll be so worried when she gets up and finds out I didn't come home last night. I leap out of the bed and pull back the curtains. Sunlight floods the room, compelling me to open the french doors. I step out onto the balcony, imagining what it would be like to live like this, to own a house like this.

By day, the view is bright and welcoming with nothing sinister about it. A wide lawn below stretches down towards the river in the distance. Over to one side, a patchwork of small fields slopes towards a grassy mound, with a sprinkling of gorse and a hawthorn at its base.

It's not big enough to call it a hill, but because of its position, it dominates the landscape and my eye is irresistibly drawn to it. It's only when I see how high the sun is in the sky, I realise how late it is and rush downstairs. The smell of freshly brewed coffee leads the way to a spacious kitchen, the white marble worktops gleaming in the sun. The others are already up. Spike is busy scrambling eggs and offers me some, while Felice points me towards the coffee pot.

"Is your father around?" I ask her, curious to meet my

employer, Axel Carr.

"No, he's away."

"Will he mind the way we all stayed over?" Mostly, I'm thinking of the mess we're making of his kitchen, and all the sheets that need to be washed.

"The cleaner comes on Monday, so he won't know a thing about it, but it wouldn't make any difference if he did. He couldn't care less." Her tone is light but there's a sullen edge to it. Something tells me father and daughter don't have the easiest relationship.

Len gulps down his coffee. "I've got to get back. The lads are going to the beach today."

"We'll come too," Felice says. "Tully will bring us over, won't you?"

"Sure." I can hardly refuse to drop them at the band's house on the way home, but I hope they'll be ready to leave soon. I'm anxious to go home before Mam gets upset.

Once again, Spike hops into the front seat. I'd prefer if it was Kit, but don't like to say anything. As soon as we turn out of the long lane that leads to Felice's house, we pass the mound that caught my eye earlier. There's a small sign pointing to it but I'm concentrating on the road and can't read it.

"What is that in there?" I ask.

"You mean the passage grave?" Felice says, while Spike murmurs something I don't catch.

"Passage grave?"

"Ancient burial site," Spike explains. "This area is well known for them."

"Oh, you mean like New Grange?" A memory comes to me of a school trip way back in primary school. We'd all been hoping they'd take us to the cinema but instead they'd brought us off to the middle of nowhere to learn about our Celtic culture and heritage. A massive stone carved with crude spirals lay on its side in front of the entrance to the burial site. It was very old, we were told, as old as the pyramids in Egypt.

In single file, we went into a narrow passage that led into a stone lined chamber at the centre of the mound. The guide explained at great length how at dawn, on the winter solstice, a shaft of light gradually enters the chamber and lights the whole thing up. We were all meant to gasp in astonishment at this early feat of engineering but none of us did. All I could think about was whether somebody had randomly spent the night in this cold creepy tomb, on the eve of the shortest day of the year, and just happened to be there when the sun came up. It seemed so unlikely, yet somebody must have done it, because otherwise how could they have figured it out?

"It's like New Grange," Spike says, "but it hasn't been all tarted up for tourists and it's not nearly as famous. So yeah, it doesn't get many visitors."

"Can you go inside?" I ask.

"Well, it has a chamber, if that's what you mean, but the Office of Public Works locked it up. Apparently it's not safe."

"Sounds like there's not much to see." It doesn't surprise me that the place isn't a busy tourist attraction but my companions fall silent. An uneasy, brooding silence, as though there's something they aren't saying. At that moment the day turns dark as a tuft of cloud sails across the sun.

"Or maybe they don't want to disturb Aonghus," Kit murmurs from the backseat.

"Who's Aonghus?" I ask.

"There are old stories about him," Spike says. "Aonghus was a Celtic god who got bored in the realm of the gods. He disguised himself as a wandering musician and set out on a hopeless quest to find his one true love in the world of men. The other gods warned him not to interfere in human affairs but Aonghus didn't listen. On his journey, he often helped couples in distress. But when he hid doomed lovers, Diarmid and Grainne, causing great war in Ireland, the gods grew angry. They cast a spell, imprisoning Aonghus in a tomb where he must sleep for eternity."

"You mean, Aonghus is in the mound we just passed?"

"It's only a local folktale." Felice's tone is dismissive, but in my rear view mirror I catch Kit flinching. She takes the story more seriously than her friend.

The sun comes out from behind the cloud and the sky is blue and bright again. The old Celtic gods are long-forgotten. There's no way one of them is sleeping in the passage grave beside Felice's house.

Spike fiddles with the car radio and, when he lands on a station playing the Black Death hit, 'Plagued By You', we all cheer and sing along.

Chapter 9

The trip back to Drimshanra seems much shorter by day. This time I find the band's house in the estate easily. They are all gathered around a van parked in front of the house as we pull up. Len shouts a greeting and everyone gets out of the car.

"I see you brought an entourage." Mac frowns at him. "Baz still isn't here."

"Relax, it's Sunday," Len says soothingly. "Baz will be down later. He won't want to miss the rehearsal tonight."

"He'd better not!" Mac throws his towel into the back of the van, and the rest of the band clamber aboard. "Jenna has him under her thumb."

"See you there!" Len waves to Felice as he climbs in beside Mac.

"Come on, everyone, hurry up!" Felice leads the way

back to my mother's car.

"Wait up," I say. "I've got to get home."

"Why, have you plans?" Felice asks.

"No, it's just my mother will be wondering where I am."

"So what?" Felice shrugs impatiently. "You can call her from the beach. She won't mind you doing something on your day off, will she?"

"No, I guess not!" Felice is right about that. Mam would be delighted to hear I was going to the beach with my new friends, so long as I can find a way to let her know. "You're sure there's a payphone at the beach?"

"Bound to be one somewhere!" She hops into the front seat before I can protest any further.

"Do you think they mind us tagging along?" I ask as we follow the van out of Drimshanra towards the coast.

"Why would they?" Felice shrugs.

"Well, you know, Mac wasn't too happy back there."

"Yeah, but that was to do with Baz and rehearsals. And Len says he's like that, always going off on one. Don't worry, the beach is for chilling, the more the merrier. Anyway, it's Sunday and there's nothing else to do."

For a moment, I'm torn. On the one hand I'm

thinking of my mother, pale and alone in the dreary house. On the other hand, it's a chance to talk to Kit again, but she hasn't said more than two words to me all morning. They are so close the three of them, it fascinates me, pulling me into their world. I've never known anyone like them before and there's nothing I want more than to be accepted by them, yet I can't tell where I fit in, or even if I fit in. All I can do is make sure they keep me around. And if that means driving them to the beach on a beautiful Sunday in July, well then, that's what I'll do.

There's a small shop near where I park the car and I go in to see if they have a payphone. Even before pushing through the door and entering the dim interior, I know it's a long shot. Turns out they don't have a phone. The only one they know of is at a hotel several miles away. Either I can drive around looking for a phone to call my mother, or I can join the others.

With a twinge of conscience I make my way down to the beach. Some of the gang have hit the water already. Felice prances around in a skimpy bikini with Len frolicking at her side in oversized beach shorts. Kit has taken off her docs, rolled up her skirt and is paddling knee deep at the water's edge.

I arrive just in time to see Mac sneak up behind her,

swoop her into his arms and dump her into the water with a huge splash. She squeals as she goes under and comes up spluttering.

I can't take my eyes off her, as she blinks the water from her eyes and shakes her hair so that droplets spray everywhere. Her dress clings to her body leaving nothing to the imagination. She's a goddess, Venus rising from the waves. Mac's cackle of delight brings me back to myself and I hastily avert my eyes. But as soon as I do, I want to look at her again. I wish I could stare at her all day.

As though conscious of the effect she's having on us all, Kit walks slowly up the beach to where Spike is waiting with a towel. I want to slap myself, if only I'd kept my wits about me, I could have been the one waiting with a towel.

I was sure Mac had no interest in Kit but he can hardly fail to have noticed her now. When he comes out of the water a few minutes later, I watch him closely, but he barely glances at Kit before spreading himself out to dry. Throwing her in the water didn't mean anything, it was his idea of a joke.

Reassured, I make my way over to sit beside her. "Would you like me to play some music for you?"

Before she answers, she glances over at Mac. His eyes

are closed and he's snoring gently.

"Sure," she says.

I take my guitar out of the boot of the car and we find a place in the dunes, away from the rest of them. The sun is shining, the sea is sparkling, and I always feel more confident with my guitar, it's like it speaks for me. Kit seems to enjoy listening, so I try something I've been working on, a piece of my own.

"That's lovely," she says.

"I can't find words to go with it. Tunes fill my head, spilling out of me, but I get stuck on the lyrics." It's not something I usually discuss, but somehow I seem to tell Kit things I've never confided in anyone else.

"How about…?" She hesitates and looks at me.

"Please, I need help."

"Okay!" She takes out a notebook. "Words come better to me when I write them down," she says a little embarrassed. "They seem to flow more easily than when I speak."

"I know exactly what you mean. I need to be playing the guitar for music to come to me."

"Well, you play and I'll write!"

Before we know it, we've sketched out a song.

She shows me the words she's scribbled.

We are the lost generation, born to run wild
Children of chaos in a dead end town
A life of desperation, disenchantment
Lost in quiet obscurity and the hidden darkness of my thoughts
Only you could cast the light, only you could turn the key
Only you could set me free.

"This is incredible." I read them in awe. "You understand music."

"No, I don't, not really. I just like playing with words. You're the one who understands the music."

"It's like a dialogue, you writing the words and me making the music. I wonder if it should be a duet." I look at her hopefully. Anyone who writes like this must be musical.

"No way! I can't sing to save my life."

Smothering a sigh, I do my best to hide my disappointment. It would have been the perfect way to spend more time together. Though I could never have written them myself, somehow her lyrics match my music. It's like there's an unexpected balance between the intensity of her words and the lightness of my melody.

"Do you mind if I work on this?" I ask her.

"Of course not." She tears out the page and hands it to me, with no idea how precious a gift she's given me. "Use whatever you want."

The dreamy afternoon passes too quickly, the waves rolling in and out in a soft summer haze. Inexorably, the tide edges ever closer and when it reaches the tyres of the van, it's time to go.

"Baz had better be back," Mac mutters as we pack up. "We need to rehearse."

"Maybe Tully can stand in, if you're stuck," Spike says, surprising me. "He plays the guitar." He must have come close enough to listen, though neither of us noticed him.

"It had better not come to that," Mac scowls. "Besides, Baz is good."

"Tully is good too," Kit astonishes me by saying. I can't believe she's talking me up to Mac Whitehead, as if he'd consider me for a moment.

"Baz will be there. I know he will."

Even though I'm expecting it, Mac's rejection still stings.

Chapter 10

By the time we get back to the band's house, I'm hoping Baz will be there. An opportunity to rehearse with an up and coming band like Black Death would be incredible, but Mac doesn't want me, and he's right because I don't know their songs and I'm not ready for it. Besides Mam will be going frantic. All she knows is I left for a party last night and never came back. With a pang I remember what happened to Spike last weekend. Mam is bound to be thinking of that too and imagining the worst. It makes me feel guilty for the nice day I've had with Kit at the beach, not that Mam would begrudge it to me, just that she's been needlessly worried.

"I should get going," I mumble awkwardly, when they all get out of the car.

"No," Kit turns back towards me. "If Baz doesn't turn

up, they'll need you. You have to stay."

She's right, I suppose. It looks bad if I just head off leaving them in the lurch. She gives me a smile of approval when I take my guitar out of the car and reluctantly follow the rest of them into the garage at the side of the house, which is now being used as the band's practice space.

Mac is in foul humour, swearing and kicking at the various cases lining the side of the shed. "The whole point of moving down here was because we need to be together. Fuck's sake, Baz skiving off to Dublin the whole time is not going to work. How the hell are we supposed to rehearse?"

It was a mistake coming in and I wish I could go. Almost as if she's reading my mind, Kit catches my eye. No one else notices the almost imperceptible shake of her head. The message is clear, she wants me to stay. Another endless ten minutes pass.

This is getting ridiculous and Mam is waiting anxiously at home. It's nothing to do with me whether Baz shows up or not, I have to leave.

Just then Len turns to Mac. "Let the kid have a go. He's up for it."

"Shit," Mac replies, slamming his fist against the

drums. "OK then. We haven't much choice, have we, thanks to Baz, the stupid wanker."

The cymbals clatter. Mac laughs, breaking the tension, and slaps my shoulder. "Let's see what you can do!"

I'm nervous as I tune my guitar. This ordeal would be embarrassing enough without an audience, but Kit, Felice and Spike are still here, determined to stay and watch. Shaking my head as I fix one of the strings, I wonder how I ended up in this mess. It was Kit who got me into it really, though she most likely thinks she's doing me a favour.

"Right," Mac shouts. "Let's go. We've wasted enough time already."

Len bangs his drums and Mac swears when I mess up the first chord. The second time I get it right and manage to fumble my way through the longest forty minutes of my life. It's awful and I cringe inside every time Mac stops to yell at me. If I knew their songs I could do a lot better. As it is, lead guitar is not a great place to play catch up. Anyway, one thing for sure is they'll never ask me to stand in for Baz again.

It should be a massive relief but I can't help feeling disappointed, like I've blown an opportunity. Despite Mac's aggressive manner, he knows what he wants from us all. I could learn a lot rehearsing with someone like him. Even in the tense forty minutes I've just endured, I've been starting to get a feeling for what it is he needs from us. There are so many ways I could improve, just by a couple of sessions with a band like Black Death, and I wish I hadn't screwed it up so badly.

"Not bad for a rookie!" Mac surprises me when he comes over and claps me on the back. "You did well kid."

He's only trying make me feel better after the abuse he heaped on me during the rehearsal. Still, for all his flaws, Mac knows how to lead, and I'm falling under his spell, just because of those few kind words. If he needed me again, I'd turn up in a heartbeat, but it's not going to happen, not after the way I messed up. I bolt out of there, too embarrassed to say goodbye to Kit or her friends.

Mam is waiting, pale and tense when I get home. She jumps to her feet as I come through the door. "Oh Tully, I was so afraid something had happened to you."

"I know, I should have called but I couldn't find a phone." It's the truth but it sounds so weak.

"Can you believe it crossed my mind to phone the police? But then I realised the first thing they'd ask me was your age and once they heard you were eighteen, they'd remind me you were legally an adult, entitled to a life of your own. And I'd just feel like a fussy, overprotective parent. They'd have been right of course, because here you are, safe and sound."

"Oh Mam!" I feel terrible thinking of the agonies she's been through. "You know I'm always here for you and I don't want to worry you like this again."

"I know, but that's just it." She comes over and puts her arms around me. "You're a good son, a responsible son, but you have your own life to lead too. I need to stop worrying and let you do your thing."

I make us both a cup of tea and she listens as I tell her about my day. At the end, she reaches over and squeezes my hand. "You're settling in so well here. Imagine, you've made new friends and you've even found a way to do your music."

Mam doesn't take music seriously, so I give her a lighthearted version of my experience with Black Death. Still, once I'm up in my room, I take out my guitar and start playing 'Plagued by You.' If I had their album, I could practise their other songs too.

The problem is I didn't start in More Video 4U until the end of June, and I'm not even sure whether I'm getting paid for the two week trial. Realistically, I won't get wages till the end of July, which is still a long way off.

After driving around all weekend, I should put petrol in Mam's car, which means there's no way I can afford the CD right now. Not that it matters. Mac Whitehead won't ask me again, so buying their album would be a waste of money I haven't got.

Instead I take out the page Kit gave me, with her lyrics, and try to work on that instead, but I can't concentrate. My thoughts turn to her as I strum idly, wondering if I'll see her again.

After the way I rushed off, without even saying goodbye, it's unlikely.

Chapter 11

The following week, Andy puts me on a split shift so I work morning and evenings, with the afternoons off. It means he gets the easiest workload and the quietest parts of the day, but I don't mind because the time passes quicker when the shop is busy.

Kit appears in the shop on Tuesday morning. "Here, I brought you this." She puts a cassette tape down on the counter. Surprised, I pick it up. It's a copy of the Black Death album, all the titles written out in her hand-writing. "Felice has the CD. She let me copy it."

"But why are you giving it to me?"

"So you can practise their songs, of course. You'll be able to learn them off the tape, won't you?"

"Yeah." Picking stuff up by ear comes easily to me

since I've never had the chance to learn music properly.

"It's a nice thought and I appreciate it," I push the cassette back towards her, "but I screwed up. They won't ask me again."

"So what's Mac going to do next time he's stuck?" She shrugs like it's obvious. "Who else can he ask? You need to be ready." She pushes the tape back to me.

Kit's not doing this to help me, she's doing it for Mac Whitehead, but she has a point. It won't hurt to be prepared, on the off chance.

"Thanks!" I put the tape in my pocket.

"You're welcome!" She saunters out of the shop, a cheeky grin plastered across her face, and I can't help smiling as I gaze after her.

For the rest of my shift, I listen to the tape, trying to figure out the chords in my head. When I get home, I stay up late in my room practising. I do the same thing on Wednesday.

On Thursday morning, the shop is quiet, just a couple of teenage girls browsing in 'Pick of the Week' with the Black Death album playing in the background. I'm in the middle of trying to figure out one of the more complex guitar sequences, when the bell pings and someone enters. I look up to see the girls frozen in shock, staring open-mouthed at the new arrival.

"Oh, you're working today?" Mac Whitehead strides up to the counter and scowls at me.

"Actually, I'm off at two."

"Great!" He brightens at this news. "So can you practise with us this afternoon? Baz can't make it again."

"Of course!" I can hardly believe my ears. "I'd love to."

As soon as he's gone, the girls flutter round me. "Oh my god, was that really Mac Whitehead?"

"Do you know him?"

"Love their music."

"He's so cool."

It brings home how little I have to offer. Why would Kit even think of looking at me when, compared to Mac Whitehead, I'm nobody? With his magnetic personality and the scruffy look that drive the girls wild, Mac is as hot as it gets. 'Plagued by You' has entered the Top Ten in the Irish Charts and Black Death is officially Ireland's most promising new band.

The band is busy getting set up in the garage when I arrive.

"Hey," Len says. The others greet me too but Mac just

sends a gruff nod in my direction.

His mood improves once the rehearsal gets underway. "Hey, kid, you've been practising."

"Thought I needed to, after making a fool of myself the last day."

"You weren't that bad." From Mac that's a massive compliment and I feel my face glow bright red.

Afterwards he calls Pete, the bass guitarist over, and the pair of them go through a few of the trickier chords with me. After a while Pete gives Mac a satisfied nod. "He's doing good, picks it up fast."

"Can you come again, if we need you?" Mac asks.

"Of course, be glad to." I write down my home and work numbers on a scrap of paper and hand it to him.

"Okay," he sticks the paper to the wall with a piece of gum. "We'll be in touch."

I drive out of there light as air, unable to believe my luck. A whole new vista is opening up in front of me. The band wants me to play with them. Sure, it's only rehearsals but, as Mam always says, one thing leads to another. Perhaps one day, if they are really stuck, I might even land a gig.

The following Monday, Mac calls me at the shop in

the morning to tell me he needs me in the afternoon. The rehearsal goes well. All the practice in my room is paying off and I know the songs by heart.

"This is our moment," Mac holds forth after the session, "the next step is the one that can take us to the big time. We all need to be on the same page. This is what we've worked for, this is what we want, and Baz is letting us down."

"He always said it didn't suit him to leave Dublin," Len speaks up in his friend's defence. "He has a job."

"He has a girlfriend," Mac replies with a scowl, "Jenna is the problem. She's the reason Baz is losing his focus."

There is no answer to that. Even if you don't agree with him, nobody ever wants to argue with Mac Whitehead. Everyone silently starts shuffling their gear together.

"What made you choose Drimshanra as your base?" I ask Mac as I'm leaving. It's something I've wondered about.

My question surprises him. "I thought you knew? This place belongs to Axel Carr. He has properties all over town. Felice got us a good deal."

Of course she did. It all makes sense now!

"The house has room for all of us and the garage is

big enough to be the perfect rehearsal space. There's no way we could afford this in Dublin. But it's near enough that we're still in the loop. Besides, it's a great base for touring at weekends," Mac goes on, almost as if he's trying to convince himself, "we need to be together, so we can take things to the next level. That's why Baz not being here isn't working. But yeah, this place is ideal."

It's true Drimshanra has a central location that works well for doing gigs in different towns in different parts of the country, but it is just a bit too far from Dublin to be convenient. Otherwise Baz would find it easier to get down, but I say nothing. There's no point in rising Mac.

Over the next couple of weeks Mac's calls become more regular. The best thing about practising with the band is that Kit starts to take me more seriously and drops into the shop more often. She spends a lot of time over at Felice's, but when she's in Drimshanra, she's only too happy for an excuse to get out of her parents' house. If the shop isn't busy, she hangs around chatting. Sometimes she even comes to rehearsals with me. The five or ten minutes in the car together, when I drive her to and from the band's house, is the highlight of my week, though all we ever talk about is Mac Whitehead.

Mac doesn't usually encourage girls at rehearsals, but he doesn't mind Kit. She takes this as a great compliment, but I think it's more he doesn't notice her. I can't say that to her though, since she's obsessed with Mac and it's hard not to fall under his spell. When he's in good humour, he has a way of making you feel special, like he's really listening to you, like you're the only one that matters. After the rehearsal, he comes over to chat to Kit and I for a while.

"Did you know Baz and I grew up together?" he asks us.

As one, we shake our heads and lean forward, eager to hear more.

"Been friends since we were kids, started our first band when we where thirteen. Can you believe that? That's how long we've been dreaming of this. In the beginning, there were three of us. The problem was we all played guitar and you couldn't have a band with two lead guitarists, so I chose Baz. Looking back, perhaps I should have chosen Joe."

"Joe?" I ask intrigued.

"Joe Killeen. He's in London now with The Good Fridays. They're doing okay. Not as well as us, though," Mac doesn't try to hide his smirk. "Still, they have a decent following over there. Joe didn't whinge about needing to stay in Dublin and work for his dad, or his uncle, or anyone else. He saw an opportunity in London and chose music. I thought Baz would do the same. But I was wrong."

Drimshanra is a far cry from London. If Black Death had gone to London for the summer, Baz might have been quicker to join them, but I keep my mouth shut.

"I can't believe the way Baz is acting, letting Mac down like that," Kit says on the ride back into town, "surely, he can see the band is the priority?"

"Perhaps Baz needs the money. Maybe he can't afford to lose his job," I point out.

"It's not the job," Kit says. "Black Death's single is in the Top Ten! They must be making loads of money."

But I'm not so sure. If they were doing so well, would they really need to live in Drimshanra to save money?

"No," Kit sounds completely sure of herself, "it's Jenna."

"Love or music," I murmur. Stealing a sideways glance at Kit, I know which one I'd pick.

One day she'll take her eyes off Mac Whitehead and look around.

When she does I'll be there waiting.

Chapter 12

A couple of weeks later, Kit asks me to drive her out to Felice's on my day off. "You can stay and spend the afternoon with us, if you like," she says.

"Sure!" I haven't been invited back to Axel Carr's house since the band's house-warming party. It's almost impossible to think that, just over a month ago, I'd never met any of them. Felice and Spike are waiting outside and we make our way across the fields to the passage grave.

Kit tells me they go there all the time. "It's our secret place," she says as we climb up to the top and I see what she means. There's a shallow dip at the top, a hollow you can't see from the ground. It's spacious enough for us all to lie there, hidden from the world.

"I can't believe nobody ever comes here." I stretch out on the grass, looking up at the blue sky. The place has a special atmosphere, quiet, peaceful, undisturbed.

"They do, sometimes," Felice says, "but there's not much to see, since you can't go inside."

"Do you think the Office of Public Works will ever open it up?"

"I doubt it," Spike shrugs. "There's talk about it, every now and then, but nothing ever happens."

"Aonghus doesn't want to be disturbed," Felice says with a laugh.

Aonghus, I'd almost forgotten about him, the sleeping god imprisoned in a stone chamber directly underneath us. In the soft summer sunshine, a tremor runs down my spine.

Before long the talk turns, as usual, to the band and Mac's continuing troubles with Baz.

"What will they do if Baz misses a gig?" Spike asks.

"That's what everyone is afraid of," I reply, "but it hasn't happened yet. Baz always turns up for the shows. It's just when it comes to the day to day stuff, rehearsals, logistics, organising everything, he can't be depended on any more."

"It's so frustrating for Mac," Kit says.

"I don't know," Felice lights a cigarette, "Mac can be a drama queen and Baz has a job and a girlfriend. Maybe the band was just a bit of craic for him, maybe he never wanted it to get serious."

"What are you talking about?" Spike and Kit turn on her. "Black Death are at the top of the charts. Why on earth wouldn't Baz want to be part of that?"

"Hey, take it easy," she throws up her hands in mock defence, "I'm only telling you what Len told me."

"Well, there you go!" Spike eyes me speculatively. "That could be your opportunity. You might get a chance to supplant Baz."

"Not gonna happen." I look down at the ground and idly pick at a blade of grass. "Jenna's going home to Kansas at the end of the summer and Baz will be back with the boys. Mac talks of nothing else."

"You know what we should do," Spike says. "We should ask Aonghus."

If there's anywhere you could imagine a Celtic god sleeping, it's here in this place untouched by time. Yet, although the prehistoric tomb is peaceful in the soft sunshine, the nightmarish visions of the first night I drove out this way linger in the back of my mind.

A sudden cloud, passing over the sun, casts a shadow

of darkness.

Kit and I both shiver.

"What's the matter?" Reaching out I give her hand a little squeeze.

"Aonghus can grant your dearest wish," she murmurs so quietly that nobody hears except me.

For an instant, I wonder if part of her actually believes the old folk tale could be true. Maybe it's something to do with growing up around here, as if the earth is permeated with its ancient past.

"No, not this again!" Felice rolls over in the grass burying her head in her hands. "Why did I say his name? Really, I thought you guys were over all that."

And yet she isn't entirely dismissive of Aonghus either. It's more of a reluctance to engage, like she'd rather shove the whole thing aside, forget she ever heard about it.

"Yes!" The idea has taken hold of Spike. "All we have to do is wake Aonghus!"

"Not listening!" Felice covers her ears with her hands.

"How do you do that?" I ask, because I too am falling under the spell of this mystical space. Once Jenna leaves, Mac is convinced everything will return to normal. That's the reason he puts up with Baz's absences.

We all have something we want from Aonghus, but it's

never as easy as that. It's true the band is on the verge of success, but it's still a leap of faith to leave everything behind to follow Mac Whitehead's dream. Even if I somehow got the opportunity to become Black Death's guitarist, would I really give up the job Mam and I depend on, in the blind hope it would all work out?

"We need to pick a special date," Spike's eyes sparkle with enthusiasm. "I know, Lunasa!"

"Lunasa?" I ask.

"Yes, Lunasa. It was one of the four major festivals of the Celtic calendar and it used to be celebrated on August 1st."

"That's this weekend," Felice says.

"Exactly," Spike says, "it's perfect."

"Like it's meant to be." It's hard to tell if Kit is pleased about this or scared.

"Lunasa was a time when the gods were well-disposed towards humanity and open to being asked favours," Spike goes on, "so it's ideal."

Under this innocuous green hill bathed in sunshine, a cold, dark passage leads to a burial chamber built in stone five thousand years ago. Could Aonghus really be in there? The thought makes me uneasy.

"We should wear flowers, bring a picnic and play

music," Kit says. "After all, Aonghus was the god of music."

"He was also the god of lovers," Spike adds, a malicious gleam in his eyes.

I do my best not to look at Kit when he says this.

"We'll have to get Len to come, so you and him can be the lovers." Spike turns to Felice.

She rolls her eyes. "We can't really ask Len without inviting Mac too."

Kit's face lights up at the suggestion. She glances away quickly, like she doesn't want anyone to notice, but I see it and it stings.

"Tully," Felice goes on, "will you tell the band?"

"Sure." It's a struggle to keep my voice level. I have a bad feeling about this party.

Chapter 13

Back at Felice's house, Spike checks the calendar to confirm that Sunday is August 1st. Away from the passage grave, in Axel Carr's immense kitchen with its sea of white marble worktop and gleaming appliances, the idea of a party for Lunasa seems ludicrous, but the others are still enthusiastic.

"Don't forget to invite the band!" Kit and Felice chorus as I leave for the evening shift at work.

I don't expect Mac will be remotely interested when I tell him about it at rehearsal next day, but I couldn't be more wrong. There's a girl he's dying to impress and a party in Axel Carr's mind-blowing house is exactly what he needs. He tells me to come round on Sunday night so I can show them how to get there. Although he loves the idea, he barely listens to any of the details, and I'm too embarrassed to get into the part about waking Aonghus.

Black Death have gigs to play down the country over the weekend so Baz and Jenna are at the house when I arrive on Sunday.

"Why are you two still here?" Mac asks them as I follow Len into the overcrowded kitchen. "You can't turn up for rehearsal but you can hang around for a party?"

"Jesus, Mac," Baz's frustrated sigh echoes around the space. "You can't just expect us to read your mind. We're trying to make an effort here."

"Thanks so much," Mac uses his most sarcastic drawl.

"You can't win with you, Mac. You're not happy whatever we do. If we're here, you give out and say we're taking advantage. If we're not here, you say we don't give a shit."

"Why do you keep saying we?" Mac's voice sizzles with anger. "This isn't about her. This is about you. You have to choose!" He jabs his finger at Baz's face. "It's us or her. You can't have both. Which is it to be?"

"Be reasonable, Mac! You know I want to be in the band and I've always supported you. But I told you there was no way I could make the move to Drimshanra work for me. It's not about Jenna, it's about my job. I need the money."

"See, that's your problem. You're looking at the small picture. If you stick with us, you'll make far more money than you ever would at that crappy job."

"Mac," Baz says evenly, "if the band is making so much money, how come you owe me nearly three hundred pounds?"

"Three hundred quid? No way. All I've borrowed is a twenty here and there."

"And the occasional fifty to fill the van?"

I shift uncomfortably. I finally got my first pay cheque and I've already lent Mac money for diesel. I couldn't really refuse when he asked me for thirty pounds for a refill. I didn't even mind. I was pleased to help out and never questioned that Mac would pay me back, until now.

"What, you'd begrudge us a tank of diesel to go to a gig?" Mac shakes his head. "I can't believe I'm hearing this shit."

"I don't begrudge it to you, but diesel is a band expense."

"Hey, look, we all take our turns," Mac says.

Baz's silence in reply worries me.

That thirty pounds would buy groceries for Mam and I for a week, or pay the phone bill for the month, and I'm beginning to think I'll never see it again. The next time Mac asks, I'll have an excuse ready.

"We're all in this together," Mac goes on. "This is a team effort. You can't pick and choose when you want to be here."

"I'm doing my best, Mac," Baz says softly. "I can't do any more."

"Yeah well, it's not enough, is it?" The threat hangs in the air and Len glances at the clock on the wall.

"Hey, Mac," he says, "it's getting late. We need to go pick up your date."

"Oh yeah," Mac smiles at the thought. "She's hot stuff."

The band piles into the van. My thoughts are jumbled as I follow them out of the estate in the little grey Honda. I can't help feeling things are reaching a climax. I like Baz and Jenna and I'd hate to be stuck in their situation, though if anyone told me I could have Kit as my girlfriend or be the guitarist in Black Death, I wouldn't need to think twice. I'd choose Kit every time, but there's no way she'd ever be interested in me unless I was in a band.

My car is behind the van so I only catch the barest glimpse of long hair and a short dress as Mac picks up his date. I haven't seen Kit since, so I haven't had a chance to warn her about Mac's new girl. I wonder what she'll think when she sees her.

I turn Mam's car around and lead the way out of Drimshanra, deep into the countryside, Mac's van close on my tail. Axel Carr's house is spooky in the twilight, at the bottom of that endless lane. There's something sinister about the sharp angles against the darkening sky, but then the front door opens in a blaze of light and Kit, Felice and Spike rush out to greet us. Kit's face falls when she sees Mac help his date, all legs and blonde hair, out of the van, but she says nothing. The band follows Felice into the house and I try to shake off my misgivings as I go up the steps after them.

Inside there's an air of excitement. Music is blaring and the kitchen is busy with preparation. The festive atmosphere turns sour as Kit watches, sullen and mute, while Mac, told what to do by Spike, carefully fixes a rose behind the blonde girl's ear. Glaring at them both, Kit snatches one for herself. Neither of them notice. Her hand is shaking as she pushes it into her hair, where it immediately topples sideways. I want to help her, but I daren't. Her lower lip is trembling and she's close to tears. Nobody else notices her anguish.

Baz and Jenna avoid each other. Jenna's eyes are rimmed with red as she helps the girls finish packing the baskets while the guys fill a cooler with beer. Mac cracks a few jokes that fall like lead in the tense silence. I wonder if he has succeeded in forcing Baz to choose.

The original plan was to walk up to the passage grave through the fields, like a procession, but Mac's date has other ideas.

"I can't walk through a field in these!" She points down at her stiletto heels.

"What size are your feet?" Felice asks. "There's probably a pair of rubber boots that would fit."

"What kind of party is this?" The blonde looks at Mac in horror.

"Hey!" He puts his arm around her. "What's this stupid shit about walking through the fields? We've got wheels. We'll drive!"

As one, the band pile into the van with all the beer.

The rest of us get into my mother's car. Kit is in the front with me while Spike and Felice are in the back, with baskets of food jammed in all around them.

"This isn't how it was supposed to be," Kit says.

"Some of these baskets are heavy," Felice replies. "Perhaps we're better off driving."

"Did you know Mac was bringing a date?" Kit asks then.

"No," Felice replies, "but I can't say I'm surprised. It's kinda typical of Mac. Why?"

Kit just shakes her head.

"Lighten up, guys," Spike calls from under the baskets that have him almost buried. "Everyone is here to party!"

None of us bother to reply. I park on the road beside the gate with the discreet Historic Monument sign and Mac's van pulls up behind me. Barely visible behind the ditch, the mound disappears into the night, anything but a party destination.

"Is this it?" Mac looks across the field in disbelief.

Laden with baskets and instruments, we struggle through the unlocked stile in single file. Even though he's never been there before, Mac leads the way up the path, his date giggling beside him. The rest of the band, Spike, Felice and I follow. Night has fallen and the basket I'm carrying is heavy in the close, humid air.

Kit and Jenna linger behind talking to each other. They've only met a couple of times, but I've noticed Jenna is someone Kit finds easy to talk to.

"I'm going back home to the US," Jenna speaks quietly and I don't want to eavesdrop, but her words drift towards me through the clammy night, "there's no point staying. Mac has driven us to this and he doesn't even care."

For a moment, the air shifts around me and the atmosphere quickens, darkens. It passes like a shadow, a glimpse of Aonghus' presence.

"What was that?" Jenna asks at the same time Baz looks around.

Before he turns away, I see the hurt in his eyes. It's tearing him apart. Mac may be his oldest friend but Jenna is the girl he loves.

In the hazy dark, on top of the ancient mound, the night should be magical, a celebration of hope and dreams, but it isn't. The band is silent, the embers of the row they had earlier simmering as their instruments lie idle on the ground.

"So what's the story?" Mac's voice is too loud and sounds forced. "What do we do now?"

The mound is quiet, sleeping, nothing stirring. If Aonghus is in there, he does not want to be woken. For a moment we all look at each other. I fumble with the case of my guitar. The undercurrent of tension is palpable. None of the band want to play, and without music, the flowers and picnic seem pointless. The night started out wrong. It was never going to be a success.

"This is bullshit!" Mac spits on the mound, quiet as a grave in the dark. "Why are we even here? This is no place for a party, let's head back to the house."

"Did you believe we could do it?" I ask Kit on the way down. "Wake Aonghus?"

She says nothing but her silence makes me wonder if she did believe it, sort of.

"It's nice to think there is something out there that can fix all your problems," I go on when she doesn't reply, "but it's bullshit."

"Yeah," she says, after a slight hesitation, almost as if she's trying to convince herself.

"Kit!" This is the moment to tell her how I feel.

"What?" Her voice is harsh, a rasp in the soft night air.

"Nothing." I shake my head and move away, glad the darkness masks my hurt and disappointment. I've been blind, hoping to win her over, and refusing to see that she's never given me any encouragement, never given me the slightest reason to think she likes me in any way other than as a friend and even then, not a particularly close friend, certainly not as close as Felice or Spike.

As we leave the passage grave, it starts to rain. First it's just a couple of drops and we begin running. By the time we reach the gate, it's lashing down and we're soaked through. At one point, everyone was going to stay over for a party, but now we all just want to go home. With a sense of anticlimax, the band climb into the van and take off into the night in a cloud of dust.

"That was some disaster," Spike says when we've all scrambled inside the car.

"You can stay over, if you want," Felice offers as I pull up at her front door. The rain has turned into a deluge and pelts against the windscreen as though trying to force its way inside.

But I can't stay here and face Kit, not when I know she's not interested in me and never will be, so I shake my head. "I'm working tomorrow morning. Thanks anyway."

I watch from my mother's car as they bolt up the steps and dash inside. None of them look back to wave me off.

Defeated, I turn the Honda around and head into the storm.

Chapter 14

There's no sign of Kit during the week. I spend my time in the shop watching through the window to see if she walks past, but she never does. Part of me is glad because I need to get over her, but mostly I miss her. Every time the phone rings, I leap to answer it, hoping for a summons from Mac, but he doesn't call. The afternoon hours between my shifts are long and hard to fill.

I find myself taking my guitar and going back to the song Kit and I wrote together at the beach, tweaking it, adding to the melody, building up the atmosphere. Some of the darker side of Drimshanra soaks into it, my misery and disappointment permeating Kit's despairing lyrics. The song matches my mood. I call it 'Dead-End Town'.

On Friday afternoon Spike bounces into the shop.

"Hey, isn't it fantastic news about 'Plagued by You?'"

"What about it?"

"It's hit Number One in the Irish Charts."

"No way, when did this happen?" It doesn't seem real.

"Today!"

I lean heavily on the counter, trying to take it in. Number One in Ireland. That's a huge deal.

"Have you heard from Mac lately?" Spike's question breaks through my amazement.

"No, not a thing since Sunday night."

"So you don't know Baz is back?"

Though I could see it coming, my stomach drops at the news. Having my worst fears confirmed hits harder than I expected. "I thought he might be."

Spike isn't fooled by my effort to sound casual. "Yeah, it's all off with Jenna. She's going home to the States."

"When's she going?"

"Don't know for sure, but she's got nothing to stick around for now."

"No, I suppose not." There's a part of me that hopes Spike is wrong, but deep down I know he isn't.

His next question surprises me. "Has Kit been in?"

"No, I thought she was staying with Felice."

"Uh no, she's not talking to us."

"What?" If there's one thing I'm sure of, it's that Kit loves her friends. "Did you guys have a row?"

Spike grimaces. "You haven't met her parents, have you?"

"No." The closest I've come is a glimpse I caught once of Mrs Lawless going up the steps of the house.

"They are really old-fashioned and strict, I mean Mrs Lawless is old-fashioned even for her generation. My grandmother is one of her closest friends, not that there's anything wrong with my grandmother, we're actually pretty close, but still…" he trails off.

"But they don't seem to mind Kit spending nearly all her time out at Felice's." I don't understand what he's getting at.

"That's different, it's the holidays, but you know they want Kit to do law? And this is her final year of school, so once she goes back, they expect her to study really hard, because law is so difficult to get into."

Yeah, even I know that. It's beginning to make sense, Kit's allusions to not being able to choose, to feeling trapped. She always seems to be doing whatever she wants, so I've never taken her complaints too seriously, or realised how strict her parents are.

"You know how Felice and Kit are in boarding school

together?" Spike asks next.

The posh school they go to in Dublin is one I'd never heard of before. Mam knew a bit about it though, told me it's very old and prestigious and Mrs Lawless had probably gone there too. When I checked with Kit, it turned out Mam was right. Not only that, Kit's grandmother had gone there too.

"I don't think Kit likes that school much," I say to Spike, "though she told me it's better with Felice there."

"Yeah, well, that's basically the crux of the matter," Spike says. "Felice won't be there."

"Shit, you're not serious!" Kit won't be happy about that. "But why not, what happened?"

"She'll still go to Saint Catherine's," Spike explains, "but she'll be a day girl. She won't be boarding any more. The thing is Axel has a cottage in Rathmines. He bought it when Felice's brothers were going through college. Now that I've got my place in Trinity and I need to move to Dublin, Axel has agreed to let Felice and I share the cottage. I'll be paying rent of course. He wouldn't mind Kit staying there and paying rent too, though it would be a tight squeeze with three of us, but we could manage it somehow."

"So, what's the problem?" The question pops out at

the same time the answer dawns on me. "Oh, Kit's parents think there would be too many distractions if she moved in with you and Felice."

"That's putting it mildly," Spike says, "but yeah, you get the idea."

"And there's no way they'll change their minds?"

The look Spike gives me says it all. "So anyway, Kit feels abandoned and blames Felice, and Felice is pissed off because she wants Kit to move in with us. It's not her fault Kit's parents are so uptight, but Kit doesn't see it like that. She thinks the offer was meaningless, since Felice knew perfectly well it couldn't be taken up."

"Jesus," I shake my head. This whole conversation is confusing me.

"Mainly, Kit thinks we should have told her about it before," Spike says.

"Why didn't you?" I ask.

"Because I only found out I got my place a couple of weeks ago and we had to be sure Axel would follow through on his promise. It's not unheard of for him to change his mind about stuff, especially where Felice is concerned. We knew Kit would take it to heart, so we decided not to say anything until it was definite."

Once Spike leaves, it hits me that Kit has been at

home all week, yet she's never dropped in once. My first assumption would be she doesn't want to see me, but after the conversation with Spike, it occurs to me she might be too upset.

Saturday is supposed to be my day off, the first Saturday I've had off in ages, but when Andy asks me to stand in for him at the last minute, I jump at it. It's not like I've any other plans and the extra money is always useful, especially since Mam isn't looking any better. She tells me she doesn't feel too bad and will be able to look for a job soon, but I'm not convinced.

"Thanks, Tully," Andy says. "Appreciate it. I owe you one."

"No problem!" In reality, Andy is the one doing me a favour. Work keeps me busy so, even though there's no sign of Kit and no word from Mac, the weekend flies by. On Monday morning, Andy throws a fifty pound note on the counter in front of me.

"What's this for?" I pick it up.

"Got a hot tip on a horse, put a fiver on it for you and the horse won! It's a 'thank you' for taking my shift on Saturday."

"Seriously?" I hand him back the note. "I wasn't doing anything else. You won this. You should keep it."

"No," he passes it back to me insistent. "Don't worry, I had a bet on for myself too. This one was for you. If the horse hadn't won, you wouldn't be getting anything."

"Really, are you sure?"

"I'm sure. Now put it away and not another word out of you."

"Wow, thanks!"

On Tuesday, Spike phones the shop. "Hey listen, we've finally managed to persuade Kit to come back out to the house on Thursday. Will you come too?"

"I can't, I'm working." I'm not sure how I feel about seeing them all again, especially Kit. She knows where to find me if she wants me, but there's been no sign of her.

"Oh no, that's fine," he hastens to reassure me, "come out after work and bring some videos!"

"Okay, right!" Somehow, I find myself agreeing even though I don't want to. Spike has this effect on you.

It's impossible to say no.

Chapter 15

Felice is particular about videos. The right film sets the tone for the evening. And she's hard to please. In the end, I bring three and hope one of them will pass her exacting standards.

"Hey, not bad," her tone is semi-impressed as she flips through them, "we could actually watch all of these."

Kit is curled up in her favourite corner of the couch, while Felice has dragged out a couple of beanbags for herself and Spike. The coffee table is piled with cans of beer and bowls of crisps. It all looks exactly the same. If Spike hadn't told me about the row, I'd never have guessed it happened. It feels awkward to get too close to Kit so I sit on the furthest end of the L-shaped couch, at an uncomfortable distance from everyone else. We munch crisps, watching the film, not feeling the need to talk. I don't want a beer, but Felice insists. "You can stay over, there's plenty of room so you can't use driving as an excuse."

I reach for a can and open it. The alcohol dulls the edges a little, makes it easier to be in the same space as Kit. My thoughts wander all over the place, drifting from Kit to Baz and how I haven't heard a word from Mac since 'Plagued by You' went to Number One. Because of the extra shift over the weekend, I haven't had a day off in ages and it's starting to catch up on me, or maybe it's the unaccustomed beer.

Towards the end of the second film, Kit falls asleep, stretched out on the couch. I get up to cover her with a throw. She murmurs in her sleep, and pulls the cover around her, nestling into it. The thought of a second beer doesn't appeal to me and, though Felice and Spike are glued to the TV screen, I can't concentrate on the film. Neither of them look up when I slip out of the living-room and creep upstairs to the spare room I stayed in six weeks ago. It feels like another lifetime.

Moonlight streams in through the french windows casting shadows in unexpected places. The night is bright and mild, drawing me to the balcony. I open the French doors and step outside. The silence creeps me out, the dark countryside stretching below me, nothing but fields of sleeping sheep and cattle, not a sound, not even the furtive rustle of a nocturnal creature.

The full moon illuminates the silhouette of the ancient burial site and casts a dull gleam on the river in the distance. As I stare out into the night, my drowsiness disappears, and I feel light and alive, sparkling with anticipation. In front of my eyes, a path appears before me, lit up by the moon. It leads straight to the passage grave.

In a trancelike state, sure I'm dreaming, I follow the shining trail. Unable to resist, the magnetic lure draws me ever closer. There's a tantalising music, a faint tinkle that vanishes as soon as you try to listen to it, but starts again once you stop. It's teasing and taunting, but I'm not afraid. All I know is I have to follow the path. It calls to something deep inside my soul, at the very core of my being. Instinctively, I obey without questioning, as if it's the most natural thing in the world to follow a glowing path into the depths of the night.

As I get closer, a darkness emanates from the tomb, reaching out and drawing me in. I can no longer see where I'm going. Someone, or something, is in there waiting for me. It's a trap and I've been caught. I'm falling, down, down, down, deep into the dark. Just when I think I'm going to hit the bottom, the darkness engulfs me.

Consumes me.

And everything goes black.

A light shining in my face wakes me up. Shielding my eyes from the dazzling beam, I scramble to sit up and look around me. A wave of nausea passes through me, and I can't tell if I'm still trapped in the strange, vivid dream. The ground beneath me is hard. Damp with dew. A torch points straight at me.

My eyes widen.

Felice.

Spike is standing beside her and they are both staring at me.

Kit is lying on the ground beside me.

What on earth happened?

In a daze, I struggle to my feet. My head is spinning and my mouth is dry.

As soon as I'm standing, I recognise the place.

I know where I am.

On top of the passage grave.

But how did I get here? And why is Kit beside me?

"Check out the lovebirds," Spike smirks.

"You scared the crap out of us!" Felice turns the torch towards Kit.

She stirs, opens her eyes and lets out a frightened moan. I help her up. Her arm is bare and cold. She shivers as she struggles to her feet. It has to be a dream, despite the sharp chill of the morning air.

Felice lights a cigarette and a trace of nicotine wafts through the crisp air. Could I smell it so clearly if I was dreaming?

Dawn is creeping over the horizon as Kit whispers something about another entrance. Her words make no sense, but Spike immediately disappears down the slope. Felice continues to stand over us with her torch. A moment later, Spike's voice comes from over the crest. "There's nothing here."

"No," Kit objects, "there is. There has to be!"

We half-tumble, half-slide down the side of the mound to join him. Kit scrabbles madly in the ground beside a hawthorn, pushing aside leaves and twigs, but Spike is right. There's nothing there. Nothing except the untouched earth.

"What are you looking for?" I ask Kit.

"The entrance to a second passageway," she replies. "It's how I found you."

I shake my head, still dazed. Everything about tonight is impossible, unless it's all a dream.

"Look," Felice says to Kit, "it's a full moon and this is an old place, loaded with atmosphere. You probably just had a really vivid dream."

"Yeah, maybe you were bewitched," Spike says with a laugh. "What do you think, Tully? Did you wake Aonghus?"

What? What's he talking about? Am I really awake? Or have they all found their way into my dream?

"I don't know." I scratch my head. "I can't remember anything. I've no idea how I got here."

"You ever sleepwalk?" Felice asks me.

"Yeah, when I was younger, but that was years ago." It's true I used to scare my mother as a child. She was always terrified I'd fall down the stairs. But the last time I did that I was nine years old, and I'm pretty sure I never went outside. Mam would have told me about it if I had.

Felice nods with satisfaction and gives Kit a 'told you so' look.

We traipse back to the house in silence. Nobody, except maybe Felice, entirely sure what to make of it all.

When we get back, Felice heads upstairs and Spike goes to curl up on the couch in the living room. Kit and I are left staring at each other across the marble-topped island in the kitchen. I hope she won't go to bed too because none of this makes any sense and I need to know what happened. When she asks me if I want coffee and goes to fill the kettle, I nod with relief.

"Did you come looking for me?" I ask.

"Yes, I saw you. In a dream. Don't you think that's weird?"

"I wish I could remember more." I rub my hand through my hair and find a bit of a leaf. Shaking my head, I put the leaf on the countertop and stare at it. "It's hard to believe it wasn't all a dream, but I guess that's the proof we were really up there."

"Can you remember anything?"

"The only thing I remember is this incredibly powerful sensation right at the end. Like I had to choose something, but it was super-important to get it right because otherwise everything would be screwed. Have you ever had one of those really vivid dreams that you're sure you'll remember, but when you wake up, it's gone? No matter how hard you try, you can't find your way back into it."

Her nod is understanding and encourages me to go on.

"Well, I guess it was like that. I still feel the memory of it there, tugging at the edge of my mind."

Something in the way she looks at me makes me feel hopeful. After all, she came to look for me, she knew where to find me. She must care a little bit. It takes her a moment to answer and I don't know what she's going to say, but when she speaks, her words are the last thing I expect.

"Aonghus was there," she says. "In the tunnel."

"Tunnel?" What is she talking about?

"The chamber? Underground? In the passage grave?"

"Kit!" I keep my voice soft, not wanting to frighten her, not wanting her to see how crazy that sounds. "We couldn't have been in there. It's locked."

"Tully, the full moon last night" she says, "that was Lunasa."

"But we already had Lunasa over a week ago." I'm totally confused now.

"We got the wrong date," she says. "The Celtic calendar followed the lunar cycle. The original festival of Lunasa was held on the night of the full moon. Changing the date to the first of August came later, in the middle ages. It was an attempt to Christianise the old pagan traditions."

"Kit?" I barely know how to ask the question, "do you think we woke Aonghus?"

"Yes," she doesn't hesitate, "don't you?"

"No."

It's the wrong answer. She turns away, embarrassed, like she was on the verge of saying something else, and changed her mind.

"I should go," I say when she doesn't look at me. "Work," I go on, feeling the need to bring us back to reality. "I have to get cleaned up."

"Does Mac mind you working days?" she asks. "You must be missing rehearsals?"

"What?" I stare blankly at the skeletal fragment of leaf on the work surface, wondering what happened last night, how Kit and I both ended up there, how much of the strangeness was a dream and how much reality. "Oh, Mac. No. He doesn't need me. Baz is back. He's broken up with Jenna."

"Mac could have been more understanding," Kit says. "They really cared about each other."

"If Baz cared that much about Jenna, he would have left the band and never looked back. That's what I'd do." I raise my eyes to meet hers, so she can see I mean it.

"Love or music," she murmurs.

"Yeah, maybe, sometimes it's hard to make the right decision." I get up to go. "Thanks for coming to find me."

She stands on the top step and watches me out of sight. Despite the exceedingly weird night, I drive into a bright new day with a smile on my lips.

She went out searching for me in the middle of the night. That proves something. Even if it's only the tiniest bit, Kit cares about me!

Chapter 16

The next day Felice and Spike stroll into the shop just before I end my morning shift. Felice dumps an enormous shopping bag on the counter in front of me. Cautiously, I peek inside. It's crammed full of videos.

Wow, I don't know what to say.

"Andy will be pleased," I murmur as I put the bag safely behind the counter, almost as if I'm afraid she'll change her mind. She has that effect on me and it's not just because she's the boss's daughter.

"I couldn't give a flying fuck about Andy," she goes straight to the point. "Have you any idea how you ended up at the passage grave last night?"

"Honestly, I don't. I went up to bed and I remember going out onto the balcony and being surprised at how bright the night was and how clearly I could see the passage grave across the field."

"You were fully clothed when we found you," Felice says.

"Yeah." I try to think back to what I did next. "I suppose I came back inside and lay down on the bed. I must have fallen asleep straight away."

"If you'd just been looking out across the field, I guess it kinda makes sense in a way that you'd sleepwalk there," Spike says rubbing his chin.

"You think?" Felice voices the doubt we're all feeling.

"Well, can you come up with any other explanation?"

"Kit thinks last night was the real Lunasa," I say slowly.

"Kit has this thing about Aonghus," Felice rounds on me, eyes flashing. "Don't encourage her!"

"But, do you think," my voice falters, "I mean, she doesn't believe in him, does she?"

"It's not so much she believes in him," Spike clicks his tongue and tosses his head, "it's more she's not sure she doesn't believe in him."

"Yeah," Felice nods, "that's a good way to put it."

"The old tales," Spike goes on, "they are rooted in the soil around here and there's always that question, isn't there? If they've endured so long, there must be something in it. Think of all the superstitions we still have, like the way we won't pick hawthorn or bring it into the house when it's in flower, or the way farmers plough around the fairy forts. Everyone knows there are things that mustn't be disturbed."

Mam doesn't bring hawthorn into the house in May either, and she has a Padre Pio medallion hidden in a recess in the car to keep us safe when we drive, but it's not the same thing. There is something warm and comforting about Padre Pio that reassures my mother, whereas Aonghus, and his associations with the full moon and ancient Celtic rituals, is much more enigmatic and scary. But then I suppose Kit, unlike my mother, isn't looking for reassurance.

"Anyway, that's not the only reason we came to see you," Felice says and I'm glad she's changed the subject. The whole idea of Aonghus, and Kit believing he might exist, is just too much for me.

"We want you to drive us to Galway!" Felice has a knack for coming out with the unexpected. "Black Death is playing a really big gig there tomorrow and we want to go. We've persuaded Kit to come too. Mac will let us all in for free if we give them a hand to get set up. So, what about it?"

"Um, I'm working tomorrow." I mean I'd like to go, of course I would, but I can't just get the day off at such short notice.

"That's a shame," Felice says, "we wanted to have a last outing together, something special, before the summer ends and we're back at school."

Now I feel really bad and I shift awkwardly from one foot to the other. "I wish I could take you. Really, I do."

"Come on," Spike takes her arm. "It's not Tully's fault."

"I'm sorry," I call after them.

"Don't worry!" Spike winks at me as he leads her out of the shop. "We'll come up with something."

I've no doubt they will, but I wish it included me.

"What's up? Why the glum face?" Andy says when he comes in to take over from me.

"It's nothing, just Felice wanted me to drive her to Galway tomorrow."

"Boss's daughter, eh?" Andy raises an eyebrow in speculation.

"No, nothing like that," I hasten to explain. "She wanted me to drive a group of them down. While she was in, she dropped these back!"

"I don't believe it," Andy swoops on the bag. "Look at all of these. We'll have an almost full inventory at the end of the month, and you know what that means?"

I shake my head.

"I've a chance at the district manager bonus. And it's a good one!" He pumps his fist in the air. "Good man, Tully. Hey, if you want to go driving the boss's daughter around the place, I can take your shift tomorrow. I owe you one and I've nothing on."

"Really?" It never even occurred to me to ask. "Are you sure?"

"Sure I'm sure. We'll be quits."

"Wow, that's fantastic, thanks Andy!"

But when I ring Axel Carr's house, there's no answer. Felice isn't home yet.

It's late by the time I finally get hold of her with the good news.

"Oh Tully," she sounds less thrilled than I expect. "We got sorted after. We're going in the van with Mac and the gang."

"Really? Is there enough space?"

"Yeah, Baz is coming down separately, so there's room for Spike and I."

Spike and Felice, I do a quick calculation. "But what about Kit?"

"Oh, Kit can't go. Her parents won't let her. It's a bummer but what can you do?"

"She must be really disappointed." I can imagine how devastated Kit feels at being left out again, even though this time it really isn't Felice or Spike's fault.

"Anyway, there wouldn't have been room for the three of us in the van."

"No, I guess not." I shouldn't be surprised at how heartless she is. This is Felice after all, but Kit is her best friend.

I put the phone down wishing I hadn't taken the day off. At least if I was working, it would pass the time and I'd earn some money, but there's no way I can ask Andy to change his plans again. Then I remember something they said earlier, about the end of the summer and wanting to do something special together before it's over.

The freedom the three of them have to just hang out and not do anything else during the endless summer days and long, sultry evenings, has felt like it could go on forever. In reality, the impromptu calls into the shop, the weekend parties, the precious moments stolen with them are all coming to an end.

In September, Kit will be back at school and I'll see even less of her than I do now. She'll still be home at weekends, I tell myself, knowing it won't be the case. Spike has already confessed he can't wait to get out of Drimshanra and Felice will have lots of new places to explore in Dublin. If they don't come home, Kit won't either.

Time is running out, but there are a couple of factors in my favour. The first is an unexpected day off tomorrow. The second is the fifty pounds Andy won for me. That will easily fill Mam's car with enough petrol to get to Galway and back. It might even stretch to lunch on the way.

Chapter 17

When I get up the next morning and go downstairs, the sun is pouring in through the window, making the dank kitchen look bright and cheerful for once.

"There's a spring in your step today," Mam says and it's true.

"Is it okay if I take the car? I might be back late."

"Have you got plans?" she asks with a smile.

"Yes, but I don't know if it's going to work out yet."

"Ah, a girl, I guessed as much. I hope she deserves you."

"Don't worry, Mam, it's still a long shot!"

"Hmm," she squeezes my arm and gives me her 'mother's know better' smile.

But once I leave the house my confidence falters. Why

put myself through this? It's never going to work. Yet, when I get to Kit's house there's a parking space just down the road. That has to be a good omen because Saturday is the busiest shopping day, and there are never empty spaces on her street. It's too close to the town centre.

Once I'm parked, I get out of the car, dust down my jeans and go up the steps. Up close, the door isn't any less intimidating. The polished doorknob stares at me like a challenge. My palms are sweaty and I wipe them on my jeans. I've come this far, what's the worst that can happen?

They could send me away, but at least I'll have tried.

I take hold of the knocker and rap firmly on the door.

A moment later, it's opened by Kit's mother.

"Hello, what do you want?"

"Good morning, Mrs Lawless," I speak in my politest voice. "I'm Tully Cabe, a friend of Kit's."

"Oh, is she expecting you?"

"Well, I was hoping to surprise her."

"She's not up yet." She looks me up and down. "But I'm sure she'll appear soon. Why don't you come in?"

I follow her through a high-ceilinged entrance hall, past an open-string staircase curving discreetly upwards.

She leads me into a poky kitchen at the back. "I'm sure you'd like a cup of tea."

I wish she'd just tell Kit I'm here, but then I realise she wants to check me out first.

"Yes, thank you," I reply hastily, "tea would be lovely."

The kitchen is old-fashioned, one side of it dominated by a heavy cast-iron range. There's a Belfast sink under the window with heavy taps. She turns one of them with difficulty and fills an antiquated kettle, which she places carefully on the range.

She waves at me to take a seat at the far end of a table covered with a blue and yellow chequered oilcloth. It should be homely and comfortable, but somehow the kitchen feels stuck, caught in a time warp.

"So, Tully, how do you know my daughter?" Mrs Lawless sits down in a matching chair at the other end.

I explain about moving to Drimshanra with my mother and finding a job in Axel Carr's video store.

"Oh yes, I remember when he first set it up. It sounded like a gimmick, another new fad that couldn't possibly last."

"This year is the fifteenth anniversary," I reply.

"Fifteen years, really? It's amazing how time passes."

I say nothing. Fifteen years ago I was three years old,

but old people measure time differently and Mrs Lawless is older than I expected, fifty if not more. It's true Mam was only twenty-one when she had me, but Mrs Lawless could easily be mistaken for Kit's granny, rather than her mother.

"Do you like working there?" she asks.

"Yes, I get to watch the videos and it's a social job, a good way to meet people."

"I suppose that's how you met Kit?"

"Yes." Thankfully, Kit chooses that exact moment to peep in the door. She sees me, gasps and rushes off, feet pounding up the stairs.

"She wasn't expecting you," Mrs Lawless laughs. "I suppose she's not dressed yet, probably hadn't even brushed her hair. Here, the tea is ready. She'll be back down in a moment. Would you like a scone?"

She pushes a plate of rather dry and unappetising scones under my nose.

"Yes, please, they look delicious."

She gives me a proper smile then and fusses around getting me a plate and a knife.

The scone tastes much better than it looks.

"This is really good, Mrs Lawless." I'm wiping the crumbs from around my mouth when Kit reappears at the door. The tentative smile she sends in my direction makes the last few minutes of struggling conversation with her mother worthwhile.

"Well," Mrs Lawless snaps at her daughter, "don't just stand there. Aren't you going to come in?"

Kit takes the chair adjacent to mine and starts worrying at a blister in the oilcloth. When her mother pushes the plate of scones towards her, she shakes her head. I catch her eye and wink at her, hoping she'll take the hint. Rolling her eyes, she reaches for a scone, and slathers it with butter and raspberry jam.

"These are good, Mum," she says, biting into it.

Mrs Lawless smiles with gratification and I seize my opening. "If it's alright with you, Mrs Lawless, I was hoping to drive Kit down to Galway today. Some friends of ours are performing there tonight. Of course, I'll bring Kit straight back here afterwards, but it might be quite late."

"Galway?" Mrs Lawless murmurs in surprise. "Gosh, I'm sure it will be very late by the time you get back from there. Kit, get your father and we'll ask him what he thinks!"

Kit darts me a look of disbelief as she gets up from the table.

"Galway," Mrs Lawless repeats, shaking her head.

Mr Lawless has a twinkle in his eye as he enters the kitchen with Kit. "So this is the friend?"

"Hello sir, pleased to meet you." I stand up to shake hands. "I'm Tully Cabe, a new arrival in Drimshanra."

"Well, I'm glad to see you've settled in and made some friends." Mr Lawless' smile is amused. He's in his fifties also, yet somehow, despite the tweeds and the pipe in his hand, he doesn't seem as old as his wife.

"They want to go down to Galway to see a show," Mrs Lawless explains. "But they're going to be back very late."

"A show?" Mr Lawless raises an eyebrow.

"Some friends of ours are performing," I put in.

"Well, I suppose we can leave the key out? What do you think, dear?" He looks at his wife for guidance. "Or I could wait up?"

"That won't be necessary, Dad," Kit says quickly. "Why don't you just leave the key out and I'll be really quiet so as not to wake you?"

Her parents exchange glances. Finally, Mr Lawless nods at me. "Very well, young man, we're trusting you to bring our daughter home safely. Don't let us down."

"No sir, I won't. Thank you very much."

"Kit, I suppose you'd better go and get ready," her

mother says. "Tully, have another scone!"

With a huge smile, I help myself, unable to believe this is really happening. It seemed like such a long shot, yet somehow Kit's old-fashioned parents have agreed to let me take their precious only daughter to Galway.

Through the window over the sink, a glimpse of the garden triggers a memory of the night of the disastrous Lunasa party, and Kit stabbing a rose into her hair. "I hear you have a wonderful garden!"

Thankfully, Mrs Lawless is passionate about her roses and that topic keeps us going until Kit comes back downstairs.

"Your parents seem nice," I say, when we finally get away. Mr and Mrs Lawless are still standing side by side at the front door, waving us off, as I lead their daughter to the car.

"You made a good impression on them," Kit says.

"Do you think so?" I hope her parents really do like me, but I'm not going to worry about that now. Kit and I have the whole day ahead together, with just the two of us in the car for the next three hours as we drive across the entire width of Ireland, from Drimshanra on the East Coast to Galway on the West.

It's all working out perfectly.

Chapter 18

Kit fiddles with the radio, searching for a station she likes. The haunting sounds of 'The Crying Game' fill the car, oozing out through the windows.

"I love that song," she says. "It captures what it's like to live in Drimshanra."

"Really? It's kinda bleak though, the song, I mean."

"Drimshanra is bleak," she says darkly.

There are worse places than Drimshanra, but I don't say it aloud. An edge of menace lurks in the streets, and it's not a place for the unwary. Yet, apart from that first night when I found Spike, I've never felt threatened by it. In fact, it's been the best summer of my life, by far.

"You all hate it here, don't you? I suppose when you go back up to Dublin in September, you'll hardly come home any more?"

"No," Kit says, "I always come home at weekends."

I try to stop a smile from breaking out across my face at this news, because it's clear from her tone she's not as happy about it as I am.

"Spike won't be here much," she adds morosely, "not when he has a new life in Dublin. And Felice will stay up at weekends too. There's always something happening in Dublin. You know they're sharing a house together next year?"

"Spike mentioned something about it," I murmur cautiously, knowing it's a sore point. "Won't you stay with them at weekends?"

"As if! There's no way my parents will let me. They want me to study hard next year, do well in my exams and get into law, so I'll be stuck forever in this hole."

"I'll be here," I say.

"Yes," the smile she gives me is genuine and lights up her face, "I'm glad I'll have one friend left at home."

"Drimshanra has been pretty good to me. I don't hate it the way you do."

"I bet you're glad to get out of it all the same, and it's a beautiful day. Can you believe we're here, in the car together on the way to Galway?" Her mood lightens as we leave the town behind. "I never thought when I woke up this morning this would happen. You're my saviour, Tully."

I grin over at her. "I'd have hated to miss the gig! You know Mac put me on the guest list?"

She doesn't answer, but I know what she's thinking. It's the least Mac could do after dropping me for Baz, but that's not how it works.

"Kit, I was never part of the band. I was privileged to get the chance to practise with them. It's the luckiest thing that ever happened to me, apart from..." Realising I'm about to say too much, I bite my tongue. "Apart from meeting you guys, I mean." I can't rush Kit. If I do, I'll scare her away.

But her thoughts aren't of me. "Felice says Mac put us all on the guest list because he needs our help."

"Yeah that's right." I don't know whether to be glad or sorry the conversation has moved to safer topics.

"But why does he need us? Surely Black Death are making money?"

"No, they're all broke. It was a bit of an eye opener when I found out." I can't help thinking of the thirty quid Mac is never going to repay me. Still, I shouldn't complain, not after the windfall from Andy.

"Broke? But they've gigs every weekend and 'Plagued by You' is Number One for the second week in the Irish charts."

"You don't need to sell that many records to top the Irish charts. And don't forget there's seven of them, plus manager and all the equipment and the van. When everything is paid for, and what's left over is divided up, it's not that much. Still they're in a great position to break through to the next level. And that's where the money is."

"What's the next level?"

"A UK Number One. That would be huge. Of course the jackpot is America, but that's a notoriously tough market to break into."

"I suppose Ireland isn't that big a deal so." Kit purses her lips in disappointment.

"Of course it is!" I want to squeeze her hand to cheer her up but I don't dare. She's warming up to me, but I need to take things slowly to stand a chance of winning her trust.

We drive in silence for a while letting the landscape unfold around us, but it isn't awkward. It's a companionable silence, each of us happy in the other's company, exchanging the odd comment about the songs that come on the radio.

The heart of Ireland is rural, its folk-tales and superstitions shaped by the ever-changing landscape and the mercurial weather. Nearly all Irish people have their roots in the country. I may have grown up in Dublin but my mother was from a farming family in Tipperary, though I've never met them. I don't know about my father, but he was probably from the country too. We leave the broad fertile, low-lying plains of the midlands behind and enter a rougher, hillier terrain.

"Would you like to stop for lunch?" I ask Kit.

"I don't mind, I'm not that hungry, but we can stop if you want to."

Her words leave me in a quandary. I was hoping to buy her lunch, but if she's not that hungry I don't want to force her to sit there watching me eat. Perhaps she's just being polite and is eager to get to Galway and join up with her friends. "Maybe we should keep going, Mac might need us!"

"Who cares about Mac? He has enough people running around after him already!"

Kit has no idea how her words make me glow inside. As the low stone walls that define the west of Ireland start to appear, I keep my eyes open, but we don't pass anywhere on the road that serves food. We leave behind the lush meadows where cattle thrive, driving through sparser ground, where sheep and goats nibble on windswept tufts of salty grass.

"Ireland isn't that big, yet it's amazing how much the landscape changes," Kit says.

"Well, the reason the west coast is so rugged is because it's bashed by three thousand miles worth of Atlantic Ocean."

"That's one way of putting it," she replies with a smile. "Do you know this road follows an ancient path called the Great Way that connected the East with the West and divided Ireland in two parts?"

"No, I had no idea. Where do you get all this prehistoric information anyway?"

"Oh, Spike dug it up on his research into Aonghus. There was an esker left along here after the ice-age and it made a natural road."

"An esker?" I muse, keen to turn the conversation away from Aonghus.

Kit prattles on about how eskers were formed from glacial deposits and how the word 'esker' comes from the Irish 'eiscir' meaning 'ridge' or 'elevation' but I'm only half-listening. I don't know what to say to her when she talks about Aonghus, sounds like she believes in him, like she wants me to believe too. It's the one thing about her that throws me off, makes me uneasy. I mean she has this fanciful, creative side that I absolutely love, it's what makes her Kit, but Aonghus is like a shadow across it.

I cling onto Spike's words. It's not so much she believes in Aonghus as that she doesn't disbelieve in him. Yet, as I follow the road alongside the ancient esker, I can't help thinking of the legendary cycles of Irish mythology – exile, destruction and lovers cursed at birth.

It's all there baked into the ancient bones of the countryside.

Chapter 19

Galway, with its brightly painted houses, in blues, purples and yellows, looks as colourful and bright as any Mediterranean resort, but I'm almost sorry when we reach our destination and it's time to join the rest of them. It takes us a while to find the Blue Ball, a venue in a converted warehouse on the furthest edge of the maze-like port.

The nearest parking is several minutes away, down a deserted side street. We run back to the Blue Ball in the blazing afternoon sunshine, and are hot and breathless when we run smack into Mac at the entrance.

"You two took your time, didn't you?" he glowers at us. "And Baz is still on the train."

"I can collect him at the station, if you want? I've got the car."

"No!" Mac shoves us inside. "I can't spare anyone to go running around after him. Let him pay for a taxi with his own money. He should have come with us. There's loads to be done."

Within the gloom of the interior, figures are scurrying in all directions.

"Hey," Len shouts from the stage, "give me a hand to get these amps in place."

"Sure!" I make my way down to join him. It's the kind of stuff I've helped with before and it comes as second nature now. Kit wanders off to assist Spike and Felice with an enormous pile of cables. Something tells me none of them have any idea what they are doing, so once I'm finished lugging amps with Len, I go over to show them what to do.

"They should have paid for a few roadies though, for a big gig like this," Felice mutters to Kit.

Everyone thinks that once you have a record in the charts, the money must be rolling in, but my time with the band has taught me that's not the case. Black Death's single is Number One and the band is broke.

There's a subdued murmur of excitement as Mac takes the stage, a lanky figure beside him. "Guess who's here?" he calls out to us.

"Hey!" Spike is hopping with glee. "Do you know who that is up there with Mac?"

I've no idea but Kit has turned pale as a ghost.

"Some big-shot talent scout from a record studio?" Felice says.

"No." Spike shakes his head, grinning from ear to ear. "It's Mike Meara."

"Really?" I can't believe it. Mac Whitehead has been trying to get hold of the legendary sound engineer all summer, but Mike Meara is notoriously elusive. "No way! Mac managed to get him in the end?"

"Better than that," Spike says. "It was Mike Meara who found Mac. He offered his help."

"Who is Mike Meara?" Kit asks.

"Only the best sound engineer in the business," Spike says.

"Yeah," I tell her. "He's worked with, like, everyone!" Mac has told us about the albums Mike Meara has recorded so many times I could almost recite the list by heart. The weird thing is any album he produces invariably becomes a classic, even though it may not be an instant hit. Mike Meara is all about music that lasts, music that stands the test of time. Of course, everyone wants him, but nobody knows how he chooses the acts he works with. Some of his clients are the biggest names in the business, but it's not about money for Mike Meara. He's just as likely to pick an unknown band and produce an album that takes them from obscurity to overnight success.

"So he thinks Black Death is going to be the next big thing?" Felice is already figuring it out.

"Mike Meara is never wrong," Spike answers.

Baz walks in at just that moment with Jenna. We all watch in silence as they make their way down through the auditorium towards the stage.

"Jeez, what time do you call this to come strolling in?" Mac roars, his face twisting into a scowl at the sight of Jenna. "What's she doing here?"

"There's something we need to tell you." Baz stops in front of the stage and stares up at Mac. He looks extremely calm and composed, even though Mac is turning red from the neck up and his eyes are bulging at the sockets. "I'm going back with Jenna."

"Yeah, I can see that!" Mac growls.

"No, I mean I'm going to America with her. On the plane. On Monday."

"You can't be serious."

"I'm totally serious."

"But this is our moment." Mac's astonishment is genuine. "Tonight is the biggest show of our lives. This is where it's gonna happen. I can't believe you're just gonna turn your back and walk out on that. We've been building up to this for years. It's the dream."

"You've been saying that all summer, Mac. Every gig is the biggest gig. Every night is the one it's gonna happen. And guess what? We're still not signed and so broke we can't even afford a couple of roadies."

"These things don't happen overnight," Mac seethes. "You have to play the long game."

"That's great coming from someone who boozes and smokes away every bit that does come in. You're so busy impressing the girls you ignore any useful contacts we make. You know what your problem is? You're afraid. You're too afraid of failure to take a chance on success."

"Get the fuck out of here the pair of you!" Mac seizes a mic and hurls it down towards Baz who ducks out of the way.

"Hey!" Mike Meara steps forward. "Take it easy."

"Mike Meara?" Baz looks up at Mac in confusion. "What's he doing here?"

"Leave, get out of my sight." Mac sounds tired as he turns away.

None of us know where to look. Mike Meara comes down the steps at the side of the stage and murmurs something to Baz and Jenna. They stumble back up through the auditorium, huddled together in a deathly silence. Baz has his arm around Jenna, helping her up the steps. The only sound as they leave the building is her muffled tears.

"You!" Mac roars as he leaps off the stage and grabs me by the shoulders. "You're on tonight."

"Holy cow!" I have no idea what else to say. The whole scene has a dreamlike quality and none of it feels real.

"You're the only one who can do it," Mac says. "You know the songs, you know the routine. You'd better not screw it up."

This is why I've done everything Mac asked me, it's why I've practised and rushed to rehearsals at the drop of a hat, because deep down, I hoped my chance would come to play with Black Death in one of their gigs.

But now I'm faced with it, I'm paralysed with fear. I'd imagined a small gig in some down-at-heel joint in the back of beyond. This is the band's biggest event of the summer, and the Blue Ball in Galway is not a hole-in-the-corner dive. 'Plagued by You' is currently the Irish

Number One, so the place will be packed out. This debut to an audience of five thousand is totally out of my league.

"What the fuck are you?" Mac yells, as though he's reading my mind. "A man or a mouse?"

"You have to do it," Kit whispers in my ear.

"Do you really think so?" I turn to her in desperation.

"Yes."

"I want to throw up, Kit. I don't think I can do this."

"When will you ever get a chance like this again, Tully? You can't turn Mac down. He needs you. Now. Tonight. And he's right. You can do this."

Her words pull me together. Yes, Mac needs me but that's not what motivates me. No, it's something else entirely.

Kit wants me to do it.

She's doing her best to persuade me.

This is my chance to prove to her I'm worthy and I mustn't blow it.

If I let Kit down, I won't be able to live with myself.

Chapter 20

Kit presses a bottle of cold water into my hands as I follow Black Death backstage to get ready for the gig. "Drink this," she says. "Take small sips and deep breaths. You'll be fine."

I wish I shared her confidence. My hands are trembling so much I can barely hold the water and I dread to think what will happen when I pick up my guitar. Backstage, nobody even mentions Baz's sudden departure or seems to care that I'm standing in for him. All they can talk about is Mike Meara.

"Fair play to you mate, I can't believe you got Mike Meara," Len slaps Mac on the shoulder.

"We just better make sure we give him a performance he won't forget!" Mac's grin is confident.

If I screw it up, none of them will ever forgive me.

Mac pulls off his t-shirt and adjusts the trademark bandana around his neck. He ties his unruly curls back in a ponytail, frowns at his reflection and pulls the hair-tie out again, shaking his hair loose around his face.

"More rockstar like that!" He catches me, reflected in the glass, watching him. "You have to get into the zone, Tully. We each have our own ways of doing it."

I'm wearing a black button down shirt and jeans. It could be worse, but I don't feel much like a rock star.

Just then Spike sticks his head in around the door.

"Hey, catch!" He throws me a pair of dark pebble glasses. They are pure Spike and not the kind of thing I'd ever wear myself.

"Put them on and get the guys to give you something to flatten your hair down. You'll rock the Oasis vibe!"

"Here!" Len shoves a tub of hair-gel at me and I rub it into my hair. The smoothed-down look isn't really me, but with the pebble glasses, there's a slick Britpop vibe going on. It's like a whole new persona, another version of myself. Mac's theory about getting into the zone is beginning to make sense.

Huddled behind the curtain, we can feel the energy building as the crowd gathers in the packed auditorium. At last, Mike Meara gives us the nod. As the lights go on and the band gets ready to burst onstage, I take a final sip of water. Mac leads the way, leaping out in front of an arena of wildly cheering fans. With a deep breath to keep the nausea at bay, I follow behind him. The others glide out after us, slipping into their places, bass, keyboard, sax, percussion and, finally, Len on drums.

Mac holds out the microphone towards the crowd and yells "Tick-Tock" and they all shout right back at him "I'm waitin'."

And suddenly, like a flash of illumination, I understand the crowd are here for us. They've come because they want to see Black Death live and they want to love us. They hope someday to tell their kids about the first time they saw Black Death, when the band was still starting out and not famous yet. All I have to do is give them what they want.

This realisation sends a spark though me and I come to life. Suddenly, I don't care! All my fears and inhibitions are gone. I just want to be here, onstage, performing. Holding my guitar aloft, I jive and jam with Mac as though my life depends on it.

As the chemistry builds between us, we take it to new heights. It's like I've found my place, my calling, and the audience can sense it. They are eating it up, loving every minute of it. The energy is electrical, charging me, and I radiate it straight back at the fans crowding the stage.

I have to do this again. This can't be my first and only time performing. Finally, I have found something that makes me feel seen.

The set passes in a blur, and I can't believe it when it's over. The last two hours have flown by on an adrenaline high. I only realise we've come to the end when Mac presents the members of the band to the crowd. "A big hand for Pete on bass, Len on drums, Maxim on keyboard, Wolf on sax and Brazilica on percussion."

Finally he introduces me. "Will you all please give a special welcome to Tully Cabe, Black Death's new lead guitarist?"

The audience roar, stamping and cheering their approval.

And I smile back at them, nodding my head, unable to believe what I'm hearing. Can it really be true? For the first time in my life I have a future. I could be worthy of Kit.

Mike Meara pops his head in backstage after the gig and Mac rushes up to greet him. "Good show, eh? What did you think?"

"Not bad," Mike says with a nod. "You did well for a

first-timer, Tully!"

Mike Meara knows my name. He thinks I did well. You could knock me over with a feather, but that doesn't stop the grin on my face stretching from one ear to the other.

Just for an instant, out of the corner of my eye, I catch Mac staring at me with murder in his eyes. But when I look again his expression is normal. It must have been my imagination.

"That was the best thing ever," I babble to Kit after the show. "I couldn't believe it. The high was unreal. I was so nervous beforehand, quaking in my shoes. Remember I wanted to get sick? But once I got out there, everything changed. The adrenaline rushes through you and you feel like you can do anything, you're the centre of the universe. It was literally like I could take the crowd and hold them in my hand."

Mac Whitehead passes by at that moment and claps me on the back. "Got a taste for it now?"

"That was the most amazing night of my life," I reply, my face still glowing.

"You did good," Mac says and moves on. His words fill me with relief. He doesn't hate me, he's not angry with me. Why should he be? I didn't let them down.

"You totally rocked it." Kit's voice is warm with admiration. "It was like you became another person up there."

"Yes, that's it, that's totally it. I felt like the person I want to be, a better, stronger, more powerful version of myself, does that make sense?"

"Yes." Her voice is doubtful, a troubled expression casting a shadow across her face.

But I plunge on. I need to tell her what I feel right now, before the high-octane confidence buzzing through every fibre of my being fizzles away.

"Kit, before I met you, my dreams seemed so far out of reach, there was no point in even thinking about them. But now they're worth chasing. Finally, I feel like I've something to live for, a purpose. You've given me that Kit. Without you, I'm nobody. Without you, I'm nothing." I look into her eyes getting lost in their green depths. Slowly her uncertainty recedes and she breaks into a smile as she looks straight back at me.

My head bends towards her and our lips meet as we kiss for the first time. It starts tentatively, but soon grows deep and passionate. The intensity takes us both by surprise. We step back and look at each other awkwardly. Everything has changed. I put my arm around her, pull her close and kiss her again. "Now this really is the best night of my life," I murmur in her ear.

Clearing up and putting the gear away after the gig passes in a haze. All that matters is that Kit is beside me and this time she doesn't want to talk to anyone else. Felice and Spike come home in the car with Kit and me. It's unspoken but we can all sense Mac wants to discuss the gig, Mike Meara and Baz's departure in private with the band.

Felice has a bunch of CDs in her bag but Mam's car only has a cassette player, so the drive back to Drimshanra passes mostly with Spike calling out instructions to Kit about what to put on the radio. Driving through the night, music on the radio and Kit at my side, this is the happiest I've ever been in my life. Among his other talents, Spike is an excellent backseat DJ and his late night music choice chills me out and brings me down gently from the buzz of the gig.

It's almost dawn when I drop them both off at Felice's house. Kit and I continue on to Drimshanra, taking the road past the passage grave. The mound is almost invisible, blending harmlessly into the sleeping countryside. Just as I'm wondering how I could ever have found it threatening or sinister, I hear a faint warning in the back of my head.

Love or music, you can't have both.

But I pay no attention. The stories about Aonghus sleeping in the passage grave are only rural superstitions.

I've had no sleep, but I've never felt so wide awake in my life. Drimshanra is peaceful and almost beautiful, the streets empty, the lights glowing like jewels, as we enter it in the small hours. I pull up at the granite steps leading to Kit's imposing front door. For once her period home doesn't intimidate me.

She pauses before opening the door of the car and we kiss again. This is real. We are a thing.

"Call you tomorrow?" I say.

"Yes." She smiles as she gets out of the car. I watch as she walks up the steps and stoops to fish the key from under the mat.

Before letting herself in, she turns to wave.

I wait until door swings closed behind her.

Then I put the car in gear and drive home through the deserted streets, a huge smile stretching across my face.

Finally, I've found a way to open the door to Kit's heart.

THE END

Continue reading...

About Mocha Von Bee

Mocha Von Bee is the author of the Kit & Tully series, which is inspired by where she grew up in Ireland, not far from the home of Aonghus, a Celtic god of love and music who's said to have lived deep inside an ancient passage grave.

Mocha loves bookshops, especially those that serve coffee and cinnamon buns, and dreams of living in Paris and taking trains across Europe.

If you enjoyed this story, please consider leaving a short review on Goodreads to help new readers discover *Kit & Tully*. Reviews don't need to be long! This one is 16 words:

"Mocha does an excellent job weaving a fast-paced and intriguing tale with eerie paranormal elements."

If you would like to find out more about the series and what comes next, you can visit Mocha online.

www.mochavonbee.com

KIT & TULLY

BOOK 2 - FIRST VALENTINE

Love or Music... Which should they choose and what price do they have to pay?

Kit finally figures out what Tully chose. And decides he got it wrong.

Aonghus might have made their wish come true, but the price is too high — a hopeless future trapped in their deadbeat hometown, unless Kit can find a way to change it. Unfortunately, there's only one way to do that. Kit needs to seek out the sleeping god again.

But now she knows the risks involved, is she desperate enough to go through with it, especially when Tully doesn't agree?

Read it next!

KIT & TULLY

WHAT READERS SAY...

Btw just wanted to say how much I'm enjoying the nostalgia on the time period. Cool Britannia, Britpop and Camden Market - love it!
@Anon

the 90s vibe is strong, and I wasn't even *alive* in the 90s. A nice subtle reminder of the story's setting!
@bigfivedonaldduckfan

You're nailing the time period, the dialog feels natural, and the characters are coming across... and now I want a prehistoric graveyard as a special place.
@guywortheyauthor

Ah, I love Ireland! What a wonderful way to describe the place
@Yamieko

I absolutely love that this takes place about 20 years ago. Such an underrated time. Technology wasn't so suffocating then, so we had more freedom, even though we didn't know it at the time. (I also worked at a movie rental place years ago, so I love that idea!)
@MarCafeWrites

Made in the USA
Monee, IL
28 April 2026